## "What does the *C* stand for?"

"I don't know." Mallory answered her girlfriend as they awaited the arrival of Dr. C. Duncan Adams. "My suspicion is that it's short for *conniving*. Or possibly *cunning*. Or—"

"I'm truly hurt," said a voice from the doorway. "After last night, I was certain you'd think I was *captivating*. You must admit I was at least *congenial*—"

"On the other hand," Mallory went on as if Duncan hadn't appeared, "it may just stand for *Casanova*."

But as she recalled the evening before, Mallory's face turned scarlet. For Duncan had behaved outrageously. He had kissed her—another man's date—in the parking lot outside the Pizza Palace in full view of *every*one.

And the worst of it was, Mallory's response hadn't been anger. Instead her blood had seemed to turn to liquid fire....

**LEIGH MICHAELS** likes writing romance fiction spiced with humor and a dash of suspense and adventure. She holds a degree in journalism and teaches creative writing in Iowa. She and her husband, a photographer, have two children but include in their family a dog pound mutt who thinks he's human and a Siamese "aristo-cat," both of whom have appeared in her books. When asked if her husband and children have also been characterized, the author pleads the Fifth Amendment.

## Books by Leigh Michaels

### HARLEQUIN PRESENTS

### HARLEQUIN ROMANCE

# LEIGH MICHAELS

## close collaboration

*Harlequin Books*

TORONTO • NEW YORK • LONDON
AMSTERDAM • PARIS • SYDNEY • HAMBURG
STOCKHOLM • ATHENS • TOKYO • MILAN

Harlequin Presents first edition September 1988
ISBN 0-373-11107-X

Original hardcover edition published in 1988
by Mills & Boon Limited

# CHAPTER ONE

THE smell of chalk dust and dry, overheated air hung in the big classroom, mixed with the pungent aroma of burnt toast and overcooked sausage. Mallory Mitchell watched patiently as her students scrambled to clean up their mess before the buzzer released them to go to their next class. While the remains of their experiment in cooking breakfast looked impossible at the moment, two years of experience in the home economics classroom had taught Mallory that it could indeed be cleaned up in less than ten minutes.

'Depending, of course,' she muttered under her breath, 'on your definition of clean!'

A tiny blonde girl, up to her elbows in a sink full of detergent suds, looked up enquiringly. 'Did you say something, Miss Mitchell?'

'Nothing important, Jill.' She raised her voice. 'Don't forget that your menu plans are due on Monday, and that there will be a test over the breakfast unit next Friday.' The buzzer sounded, cutting off groans from a couple students.

'A test next week? Already?' one of them moaned as he flung his dish towel towards the rack and rushed to pick up his books from the far end of the classroom.

'That's what I said, David.'

'Come on, Miss Mitchell. What could you possibly ask us on a test? How to boil an egg, for crying out loud? Everybody knows that.'

'Think positive, David,' Mallory recommended crisply. 'Since you're certain that you already know everything

5

there is to know about breakfasts, it should be a very easy test. I'm sure you'll get an excellent grade.'

David groaned again, but he didn't pursue the subject. It was just as well, Mallory thought, since sarcasm in the classroom was officially frowned upon. David was, at the moment, in danger of failing cooking class.

The classroom was empty in a matter of seconds, leaving only Mallory and the slim blonde who was rinsing the sink with painstaking care. 'Thanks, Jill,' Mallory said. 'But don't be late to your next class.'

A tall, dark-haired boy in jeans and a striped sweater poked his head in the door. 'Hi, Mallory.'

Mallory looked at her younger brother in surprise. 'What are you doing here, Matt? You normally avoid this room like the plague during school hours, unless you forgot your lunch money.'

Matt Mitchell grinned. 'Sorry to disappoint you, but I remembered it today. Ready, Jill?'

The girl seemed to glow, as if a flame had been turned up in her eyes. Well, Mallory thought. So she thinks my little brother is something special!

'Don't forget you'll be on your own for dinner tonight,' she reminded Matt. 'I'm going to that faculty-student council dinner with Dad.'

Matt made a face. 'I suppose I'm having leftovers again?'

'Unless you want to cook, yes. And if you make any more fuss about it, next time I'll suggest that Dad ask you to go with him instead of me,' Mallory threatened.

'He wouldn't. You fit much more nicely into the college community than I do. See you later, Mallory.' The two students went off down the hall, with Matt carrying Jill's books. It was the first time Mallory had seen that happen, too, and she made a mental note to keep a closer eye on Matt. Those two kids, at sixteen, were barely more than babies . . .

She stopped in the office, and was looking through the contents of her mailbox when the principal's secretary said, 'I'm afraid Mr Craig is tied up with a luncheon meeting today, Miss Mitchell.'

Mallory was startled. She hadn't realised that she and Randy Craig had been having lunch together often enough to excite comment, but obviously someone had noticed.

And what of it? she asked herself. They weren't trying to keep anything secret. She and Randy had dated occasionally in the last year, since his divorce had become final. It certainly didn't interfere with their jobs. Sometimes it was almost a part of the job—as when they chaperoned the school dances. They'd got into the habit of going together, because it made a boring job much more pleasant. If that bothered anyone—Mallory shrugged and dismissed the thought.

There was a slim envelope in her mailbox, with a return address that sent shivers down her spine. McDaniel Publishing House, it read in block letters.

'On your way to the cafeteria, Mallory?' a cheerful voice asked behind her.

'Hi, Melinda.' Mallory stuffed the letter down into the side pocket of her handbag. There would be plenty of time to look at it later, without an audience. Not that Melinda wouldn't be delighted if the news was good, but just in case it wasn't, Mallory was determined not to make it public. She had gone to great lengths to make sure no one at the high school would know what she was up to, and she wasn't about to let the secret out now. 'Want to sit with me?'

'Of course. Pleasant company makes even cafeteria food taste better.' Melinda Anderson handed a packet across the counter to the secretary. 'I'll need thirty copies of that next week.' She held the door for Mallory. 'Though I'm amazed that you eat in the cafeteria,

Mallory. With all that real food right in your classroom——'

'Believe me, Melinda, by the time my cooking students
get done with it, it usually doesn't look very appetising.'

'Well, it certainly smelled good this morning. Do you
have any idea how difficult it is to pound algebraic
equations into the heads of a bunch of freshmen when
the smell of sausage is wafting through the air?'

Mallory smiled. 'I'll keep that in mind when I make
up my next menu.'

'I have an even better idea. For your final exam, why
don't you have a beef Stroganoff contest? I'll judge.'

'That's an idea.'

Melinda looked doubtfully at the taco on her tray.
'Do you know, every time in the last few days that I've
tried to eat, I find myself remembering the wonderful
taste of your Stroganoff last weekend.'

'Would you like the recipe?'

'Of course, but I doubt I could pull it off as well as
you do.'

'There's really nothing to it.' Mallory bit into her taco.

'Right. Every expert says that, and then looks astounded when the average person can't do it.'

'Well, I must admit to some frustration with beginning cooks these days,' Mallory admitted.

'Getting disillusioned with the job already?' Melinda
commiserated. 'You've only been at it for two years.
Wait till you've been here seven, as I have.'

'But cooking and sewing are so easy, Melinda, and
yet these kids botch it up. They just don't seem to have
any common sense.'

Melinda said wisely, 'If you expected common sense,
you shouldn't be teaching in high school. I don't think
it's teaching anyway, Mallory. I think you'd be happier
if you had a husband and a home of your own.'

Mallory stared at her friend in astonishment. 'And you call yourself a liberated woman, Melinda!'

'I just meant that you've got all the responsibilities of an old married lady, with none of the fun.'

'Do you mean Matt?'

'Who else would I be talking about? You don't have any other little brothers locked in cupboards, do you?'

Mallory smiled. 'Sometimes I'd like to lock him up, that's sure. Well, two more years and Matt will graduate and be out on his own. I'll just have to hold out till then.'

'You could at least look around. There are a few eligible men in this town.'

'Yes, and I dated them all while I was in high school. Do you know how hard it is to feel romantic about someone that you remember as a teenager with braces and acne?'

'I see your point,' grimaced Melinda.

'In the meantime, my senior living class will keep me sane.'

'Your experiment is going well, then?'

Mallory glanced around the room, and lowered her voice. 'So well that I don't want to tell the people in the social studies wing about it, or they might take the kids away from me.'

'And why should they want to, pray tell? They're the ones who told Randy Craig that the whole idea of a class to teach kids how to live on their own was a waste of time.'

'But if it's a success, Melinda, it will draw attention. And then——'

'I see what you mean,' Melinda said ruefully. 'The social studies people will want to take the credit, and they can't do that if you're teaching the course.'

'Right.'

'Faculty in-fighting,' Melinda said with disgust. She pushed the remains of her taco aside. 'Why can't we all just remember the simple fact that our goal is to educate kids here, not to climb all over each other's egos?'

'Find the answer to that and they'll make you the boss.'

'Heaven forbid!' Melinda said, unabashed. She hurried across the cafeteria to hand her tray back into the kitchen.

Mallory glanced around the room. The noise level had dropped as the crowd thinned. Spring was coming near, and it was warm enough today that many of the students had stepped outside for a breath of fresh air before going back to class. Another five minutes and the next group would flood the cafeteria with noise and high spirits for their short break.

But in the meantime, it was safe enough. No one was paying any attention to her. She casually pulled the crumpled envelope from her handbag and slid her fingernail under the flap. Her black hair spilled forward over her face as she read the letter.

It was only one page, brief and to the point. The editors had found her proposal a fascinating one; to the best of their knowledge no one had yet written a textbook for a course intended to assist high school students to make the transition from teenage family member to independent adult. Her outline, they felt, was quite comprehensive, covering as it did everything from renting an apartment to buying car insurance to coping with loneliness, and they thought such a book would have a large possible market.

But—Mallory's heart sank—the editors must express a doubt as to whether a book of this sort, written by an unknown high school home economics teacher, would have the credibility necessary to sell it on a wide scale. And, of course, unless a great many schools used the book, it would be impractical to produce it. Of course,

she must realise that such a textbook involved more sociology than anything else, and that it did not properly
belong in the home economics division at all.

Perhaps a qualified sociologist would agree to co-
author the book, the editors went on. Without such an
authority, they very much regretted having to say that
the book would probably not be worth her time to
complete...

'Damn,' Mallory muttered. The buzzer sounded, and
she crumpled the sheet of stationery back into her bag
without bothering to read the rest of the letter. She
struggled down the hall towards her classroom, against
the wave of hungry teenagers headed for the cafeteria.

'A co-author,' she muttered. 'I don't want anyone else
messing about with my book. It isn't fair, anyway. I'm
the one who developed the course. I wrote the teaching
plans. I did the research. But just because I'm not a
sociologist with an advanced degree, they won't even talk
to me!

'Not worth my time to finish,'she muttered. Of course,
what the editors hadn't known was that the book was
already nearly complete. Since she had never tackled a
project quite that large before, Mallory had hesitated to
promise something she wasn't certain she could deliver.
So she had written the book first, and then sent the
outline. There was a three-inch-thick stack of neatly
typed manuscript in her desk drawer at home, just
waiting for a positive reply. And now this, telling her
that all her work had been wasted.

She taught her advanced sewing class, and wrote the
test on breakfasts for her beginning cooks. But not even
the last hour of the day, when her prize seniors burst
into the room to share what they had learned about life
insurance from talking to an agent, perked up her spirits.

*Not worth your time to finish*. The refrain ran through
her mind throughout the afternoon. Well, Mallory

thought, we will certainly see about that! It's a good book, and it shouldn't matter whose name is on the title page.

Matt was playing ball in front of the garage when she pulled her little car into the driveway beside the steep-roofed red-brick house. Mallory tapped the horn and waited till he'd retrieved his ball and got out of her way. She parked the car and lifted a briefcase full of papers from the back seat. 'I thought you were working on the play after school,' she said.

'They had plenty of help. Didn't need me.' His shot bounced off the wall, and he chased it. 'Besides,' he grinned, 'Jill felt sorry for me and invited me over to her house for dinner.'

'Scavenger,' Mallory said, and went into the house.

Her father was in his little study at the back of the house, the small hideaway that had once been a maid's bedroom. Now it was panelled in fine wood and lined with shelves loaded with books and pamphlets. A desk-lamp cast a pool of brilliance over the blotter, where a book lay open. Professor Mitchell was taking notes. He was so absorbed in his task that he didn't hear Mallory come in.

She watched him for a minute, his thinning silver hair shining in the glow of the lamp as he bent over his task. 'Did you find a new resource?' she asked, finally.

He looked up, startled, his eyes bright over the half-lenses of his reading-glasses. 'Mallory! You're home early.'

'Sorry, Dad, but you can't have looked at a clock lately.'

The professor pulled a gold pocket-watch out. 'Oh!' he said. 'And we have a dinner date tonight, don't we?'

Mallory nodded. 'That's why I came in to check on you—I suspected you might forget all about dinner. It must be a fascinating book.'

'Yes, it is.' His voice was as eager as a boy's. 'Another of those amateur scholars who insists that Shakespeare couldn't possibly have written all those plays, and who thinks that his half-baked beliefs constitute proof! I waste half of my time at lectures, you know, refuting all of these unfounded theories that masquerade as fact. It's beyond me to know why so many people believe that Shakespeare must have been some kind of fraud——'

'I know, Dad. He was simply a genius who wrote for the popular taste and had no idea at the time that he was writing classics.'

The professor smiled. 'I've bored you with my views before, is that what you're telling me?'

'I'm not exactly bored, Dad.' She picked up the book and flipped through the pages. 'This isn't even commercially printed, is it?'

'No. He had to publish it himself.' Professor Mitchell sounded triumphant. 'Nobody would back up his ideas with money to distribute them.'

'Well, it isn't only amateur Shakespearean scholars who can't find a publisher.' Her tone was distant.

The professor's eyes were suddenly sharp. 'What happened, Mallory? Was your book turned down?'

'Not exactly. Here—read this.' She handed her letter over and perched on the window-seat while he read it. She rested her forehead against the leaded windowpanes and looked out across the wooded ravine behind the house. Here and there a haze of green was beginning to show on the trees, and the grass was already showing a promise of spring. A few more days of this warmth, she thought, and the tender new leaves would burst forth. It would be an early spring, after a cold and harsh winter. How she longed to get out into the woods, to pack a picnic lunch and go biking, to walk through the grass and feel the blades tickling against her toes, made tender by a winter protected by shoes——

It's too early to get spring fever, she reminded herself. There are still two months of school before you can call your time your own.

The professor put the letter down on his desk blotter and looked up, pulling his glasses off. 'Well, I don't quite see why they want a sociologist. That would never have occurred to me.'

'Me neither,' Mallory muttered.

'But on the whole, I'd say it's a very positive answer.'

She shrugged. 'I suppose so, if I agree to collaborate with some so-called expert. Dad, it's my book! I've done all the work. Why should I have to turn it all over to someone else? I feel like a child being told that I'm not smart enough to finish this project by myself.'

'Would you rather have it not published at all?'

Mallory stared out of the window. 'No,' she said softly. 'I think there's a need for it.'

'So do I, dear. Don't worry, we'll solve the problem. All you need, actually, is the name. It's done all the time. If you saw the list of books some professors' names appear on, you'd think they never had time to teach a class. The truth is, they didn't have anything to do with writing the books.' He smiled reassuringly at her. 'All you need is somebody who sees the value of what you've done, and who has the credentials you lack.'

'You make it sound so easy.'

'It may be. There's one man in particular I'm thinking of. With his name on the cover——'

'You know someone? You're a genius, Dad, the answer to a maiden's prayer.' Mallory jumped up, new enthusiasm welling up in her. 'Give me his address, and I'll write to him this minute.'

The professor's brow wrinkled. 'Why bother?'

'You aren't suggesting that I do anything without asking his permission are you?'

'Of course not!' The professor sounded horrified. 'That would be unethical. I merely meant that you could ask him at the dinner tonight.

'He'll be there?' Mallory was startled.

'Of course. He's the head of the sociology department at Chandler College, and that automatically puts him on the faculty-student council.'

'What incredible luck,' Mallory murmured. She kissed her father's cheek. 'Have I ever told you what a wonderful pal you are, Dad?'

'I know I am,' the professor said modestly. His eyes strayed to his book, open on the blotter. 'Do you suppose I have time to read one more chapter before I get ready for dinner?' His tone was wistful.

Mallory laughed. 'I'll drag you out of here fifteen minutes before we're due to leave,' she promised, and went up to her own room with a lighter heart. For the first time in her life, she was actually looking forward to attending a college function with her father.

It took Professor Mitchell a bit more than fifteen minutes to dress, so they were late when they reached the student centre where the faculty-student council held its meetings and dinners. The professor took the stairs two at a time on his way to the dining-room, but on the landing Mallory stopped and tugged at the sleeve of his sports jacket. 'Would you slow down?' she asked breathlessly. 'You're making me look bad. And you didn't even tell me his name.'

'Whose name?' He looked confused.

For a moment she was furious. This is no time to be the absent-minded professor, Dad, she was thinking. 'Your friend who is going to help with my book,' she reminded crisply.

'Oh!' The professor's brow cleared. 'Adams. C. Duncan Adams.'

Sounds like a stuck-up scholar, Mallory thought. Anyone who used an initial instead of a first name impressed her as a snob. 'What does the "C" stand for?'

Her father grunted 'I'm not sure. "Conspicuous" perhaps—he's certainly well-known.'

Mallory decided it didn't make any difference what the man called himself. Perhaps his mother had named him Clyde, and he was trying to assume an image a bit more attractive to his young students. Her own father's given name was Harold; many of the men of his generation had been christened with names that their children now considered to be hilarious.

'I don't see him, though,' Professor Mitchell said. He craned his neck to see who was on the far side of the room. 'Perhaps he's just late.'

'We're the ones who are late,' Mallory pointed out. 'They are already setting up the buffet line. Anyone who's later than we are is simply not coming.'

'Well, that's possible, too,' the professor conceded. 'I know he hates these things. Would you like a drink?'

'A glass of wine. Dad?' She caught him as he started to turn away. 'Would you tell me what he looks like, at least? Then I could be looking for him.'

'Oh. He's taller than I am,' the professor offered helpfully.

'Dad, half the men here are taller than you are. Come to that, a good dozen of the women are taller——'

'Mallory, there is no need to be insulting about my lack of height. Duncan's kind of loose-limbed, too——' His attention was distracted by a colleague. 'Jim! Good to see you, pal. How's that project your grad students are doing?'

The two men moved away, and Mallory sighed. I don't know why I bother to come to these things, she thought. As soon as we're inside the door, he forgets I'm here, and spends the rest of the evening wandering from one

old friend to the next. I'm left to look out for myself,
and nine times out of ten I have to remind him I'm here
when it's time to go home.

In the three years since her mother had died, Mallory
had decided at least a dozen times that she would never
again accompany her father to an official college
function. Yet, every time he asked her to go, it was with
an air that implied he'd be a lost puppy if she didn't
come with him. And so she went.

'Next time it's Matt's turn,' she muttered under her
breath. She surveyed the crowd. A tall, loose-limbed
man, hmmm? Well, there were several who qualified,
but she could hardly walk up to each in turn and ask if
he was the brilliant sociologist she wanted to ask a favour
of. Now if there had been one dressed in a safari-type
jacket, as if he'd just come back from studying the
aborigines...

Dad could at least have told me what colour the man's
hair is, she thought irritably. She decided to get herself
a glass of wine. Mallory had learned to look out for
herself. If the event ran according to past pattern, the
professor would already have forgotten his offer to get
her one. In fact, sometimes he even forgot to eat at these
affairs and arrived home absolutely famished and not
quite sure why he should be hungry.

Tonight there was a huge tray of tiny meatballs in a
spicy barbecue sauce at one end of the table. They looked
good, and Mallory put her wine-glass between two
fingers so she could hold a paper plate as well, freeing
her other hand to serve herself. It was a skill learned
long ago at buffet dinners.

She placed several tiny meatballs on to the edge of
her plate and covered them with a spoonful of sauce.
Usually, if she had enough of a taste, she could deduce
how the sauce had been concocted. She could have the
recipe, of course, by merely calling the student centre

tomorrow where the cooks were who had produced the food, but it was more of a challenge to figure it out herself. Besides, she had found that analysing the food helped to fill up a long evening, if there was no one interesting to talk to.

On the other side of the table, a dozen feet from Mallory, a man gestured with his plastic glass and said, 'On the contrary, my dear man. The research in Samoa has been shown to be faulty, but it was hardly a fraud! The natives showed a disturbing tendency to do what the researchers seemed to want them to do, but after all, that's only human! It's one of the things we are always fighting in sociological research——'

Mallory stood up a little straighter. That's him, she thought. That's got to be him. How many men in this crowd are going to be talking about the problems of sociological research in Samoa?

She tried not to stare at him. She stole glances from under her dark lashes as she spooned food on to her plate at random. C. Duncan Adams was certainly tall. Loose-limbed—well, she supposed that was a matter of judgement. She would have called him awkward, instead. Now, she just had to figure out how to approach him.

'Excuse me,' a polite voice said at her elbow. 'I was just wondering if you're serving yourself, or planning to take up residence here?'

'Oh,' she said. 'Sorry.' She put a forkful of macaroni salad on her plate and glanced at the next bowl. Minced cucumbers, she thought, with some kind of sour cream dressing. Absently, she reached for the spoon, and stole another look at C. Duncan Adams across the table.

He was swinging his arms around as he talked; that must be what the professor had meant by loose-limbed. He looked like a pelican flapping its wings. He was also slightly red-faced, and his tweed jacket was baggy at the elbows. The home economics teacher part of her longed to take it away from him and press it.

'At any rate,' the man was continuing, 'researchers are just going to have to be more careful in the future. There aren't any isolated groups to study any more, as there were at the turn of the century.' He pulled up his sleeve and looked at his wristwatch. 'But I've got to be going. Nice to see you——'

He can't leave now! Mallory thought. I have to catch him. I can't let him get away——

She broke out of the serving line at the table, determined to catch C. Duncan Adams before he escaped. Her paper plate, never intended to hold up under the load of food she had absent-mindedly piled on it, buckled, and the wine-glass slipped from between her fingers. White wine, macaroni salad, meatballs with sauce and cucumbers in sour cream cascaded in a stream down the front of the neatly tailored wool jacket of the man beside her.

He glanced at the mess, which dripped from the jacket down his crisply creased trousers and to the floor, and then looked coldly at Mallory.

'I am sorry,' she whispered. 'It will have to be cleaned. I'll pay for it, of course——'

'Oh, here you are,' a cheerful voice broke in. 'Here's your wine, Mallory. My boy, what happened to your jacket?' Professor Mitchell looked startled.

If he can't see, Mallory thought, I'm not going to try to explain.

But the cheerfulness was back in the professor's voice. 'I see you've met,' he said.

'Met?' the macaroni salad man said. The word was chopped off as if he didn't trust himself to say more.

'Yes,' Professor Mitchell went on. 'Or shall I make it formal? Mallory, this is Duncan Adams. Duncan, my daughter Mallory.' Then a note of concern crept in. 'Mallory?' he said, 'Are you all right, dear?'

# CHAPTER TWO

HER father's question brought one option to Mallory's mind. She could stagger a little, pretend to faint, and fall down. Maybe everyone would charitably assume that her clumsiness had been only a symptom of some sudden illness.

But she couldn't think of a graceful way to hit the floor, and she suspected that no one would intervene to catch her. Her father would be too stunned to try to do anything, and as for C. Duncan Adams—well, he would certainly not put himself to any trouble to break her fall. Or to pick her up, either—he'd probably just step over her as she lay there in the macaroni salad. No, falling down would only make things worse. The only option was to admit the truth.

She stole a look up at the man beside her. It was no surprise that she had passed over him in her search; while he was certainly tall, he wasn't out of the ordinary, and she could detect no other resemblance to the person her father had attempted to describe. Besides, wasn't he simply too young to be not only a full professor but the head of the department? She had been looking for a man in his fifties, a grey-haired scholar. This man was in his middle thirties, with impatient coffee-coloured eyes and honest-to-goodness golden-blond hair.

I'll bet your female students are more interested in you than in sociology, Mallory thought. And that probably accounted for the impatience, too; a man like this would expect to be treated with deference.

A blonde woman in a glittery red dress hurried up to him. 'Duncan!' she cooed. 'What on earth happened to you? Let me brush you off——'

'Leave it, Caroline,' he said brusquely. 'No amount of brushing will make any difference. I'll have to go home and change.'

Ah, Mallory thought. And here we have Mrs Adams—she must be his wife, because no man who wasn't married to her would use that tone of voice to someone as gorgeous as she is.

'Have you asked him?' Professor Mitchell questioned.

Mallory sighed. 'No, Dad,' she said, trying to be polite, even though she wished her father would just take himself off and not make things even worse.

'Do you mean you were attempting to start a conversation with me?' C. Duncan Adams said. 'You certainly have a unique way of getting a man's attention.'

'I am sorry, Mr Adams.' She caught herself. There was nothing like adding insult to injury by ignoring his title! 'Professor Adams—Dr Adams——'

'Why don't we settle on "hey, you", and I'll promise to get out of your way whenever I hear you coming?'

Mallory's initial embarrassment was beginning to vanish under the weight of anger. After all, she thought, it had been an accident! She summoned her dignity. 'There was a matter I wanted to discuss with you, Dr Adams.'

His eyebrows arched. 'If you think I'm going to stand here, while mayonnaise soaks through my clothes, and listen to some cockamamie scheme——'

'It's not mayonnaise. It's sour cream,' Mallory volunteered.

'How would you know?'

She regretted opening her mouth at all. What difference did it make? 'I just know. Food is my business...' Her voice trailed off.

'Yes, I can see that you have a great fondness for it.' C. Duncan Adams turned to the blonde woman at his elbow. 'I'll be back to pick you up later, Caroline.'

She tucked a small hand into his arm. 'I'd rather come with you now, Duncan,' she murmured. Her voice was intimate. She sounded a little shy.

Mallory took a step forward. 'Can I at least take your jacket to the cleaners, Dr Adams? It was my fault, after all——'

'No thanks, it would probably come back in shreds. I'm particularly fond of this jacket; I wouldn't like to risk it.'

She couldn't blame him for being angry, of course. Mallory watched as he and the gorgeous blonde left the room, and sighed. So much for that hope of getting help with her book. She'd crushed it herself, and she had no one else to blame.

She turned to her father. 'Do you have any other old friends who have doctoral degrees in sociology?' she asked hopefully.

The professor shook his head. 'No. Besides, Duncan's credentials are the best. I really think you'd better try to make up with him, Mallory.'

'After that?' Mallory asked. 'You must be kidding. He'll never listen to anything I say.'

'Why not? It was an accident.'

'Somehow,' Mallory murmured, 'I don't think Dr Adams is likely to understand that.'

Professor Mitchell didn't let it rest there, however. On the way home, he told Mallory about C. Duncan Adams' list of accomplishments: books he had written, research he had published, breakthroughs he had made.

Mallory was unconvinced. 'If he's so wonderful,' she asked sceptically, 'why is he at Chandler College? This is a nice town, but it's hardly the big time.'

'Mallory, surely you know the answer to that. At a small college, a professor can work more closely with his students. He gets to know them individually, not as a mass of faces in a lecture hall. And I suspect Duncan's working on a project at the moment, something for which he needs the quiet atmosphere of a college town.'

'Then he probably wouldn't have time for my book, anyway.'

'That's possible. But you'll only find out if you ask.'

'There must be someone else who could help me.'

'No one as good as Duncan.'

Mallory was getting a little tired of hearing her father singing C. Duncan Adams' praises. 'You know, Dad, this whole thing tonight was your fault,' she said.

'Mine?' He sounded horrified.

'That's right. If you'd told me all these things before we got to the dinner, I wouldn't have made the mistake I did. There was another man that I thought was Clyde——'

'Clyde?' There was confusion in his voice. 'Who's Clyde?'

Mallory coloured a little. 'That slipped out. I was just wondering about the initial, you see, and I thought perhaps your paragon's first name was actually Clyde. That's it, Dad—that's the answer!'

'Clyde?'

'No. The other man I thought must be your famous Dr Adams. He was talking about research in Samoa, and so I naturally assumed——'

'What did he look like?'

'Tall and loose-limbed,' Mallory snapped, and then relented. 'He was red-faced and wearing baggy tweeds.'

The professor's face cleared. 'Oh, that's Ernie Ryan.'

'Well, if he has a degree in sociology——'

'He doesn't. He teaches freshman composition, and when he's in his cups he thinks he's an expert on everything. He knows less about Samoa than I do.'

'Oh.' Mallory was momentarily downcast. 'Well, there are other universities. I can write to some people——'

'Don't be such a chicken-hearted defeatist, Mallory,' the professor said crisply. 'Duncan doesn't know anything about your project yet. He certainly doesn't know how much time you've put into this. At least call and talk to him before you give up. Isn't your book worth that much effort?'

She thought about that all the following day. She taught her classes with only half her mind on the subject. The other half was thinking about her book. Was she just being chicken-hearted, as her father had accused, if she avoided facing C. Duncan Adams again?

Finally she concluded that there would be no peace at home until she could give her father Dr Adams' final answer. So after school she stopped at home just long enough to retrieve her manuscript, and then drove over to the college as fast as she could, giving herself as little time as possible to back out.

It wasn't hard to find his office, on the second floor of the old red-brick liberal arts building. But it was midterm, and students were lined up outside the rows of offices, waiting to see professors. Dr Adams' office was no exception, but Mallory noted with grim humour that there was an extraordinarily high proportion of young women in the crowd outside his door.

She found a place to sit on a wide windowsill, and hugged her manuscript close, as if hoping that it would protect her and keep her courage up while she waited.

Nearly an hour passed before her turn came. By then the halls were quiet, and several of the professors had locked their doors and left. The last student came out of Dr Adams' office and turned towards the stairs. Mallory stood up, clutched her manuscript, and took a deep breath.

The students hadn't bothered to knock; they had just gone in one at a time. But Mallory didn't feel quite comfortable with doing that. She tapped hesitantly on the doorjamb and peeked around it.

'Come in,' he said, without raising his head from the papers on his desk. 'Why did everyone choose today to have problems? What sort of trouble are you in?'

'Plenty, I'm afraid,' she said.

His pen stopped in the middle of a word, as if it had suddenly frozen in his hand. Very slowly, he looked up. 'I thought I couldn't be mistaken about that voice,' he said. 'I'm sorry, but my office hours are over for the day. If you will excuse me——' He put the pen down and reached for his briefcase.

Mallory stood her ground. 'According to the sign beside your door,' she pointed out, 'your office hours were over thirty minutes ago. I'd like to have two minutes of your time; that's all I'm asking.'

He sighed and set the briefcase down. He walked over to the window, as if studying whether it was possible to escape that way. Then he looked at his watch and said, 'Start talking.'

Two minutes later, when Dr Adams held up a hand to stop her, Mallory was completely out of breath. But she protested, 'I've hardly started. Please, you have to let me finish——'

'Then you should have asked for more than two minutes,' he said. But there was no cutting edge to his voice. 'Look, Miss Mitchell,' he said, 'I've never worked with a co-author. And I certainly am not about to spend valuable time on a book that was not my idea and that may or may not even sell——'

'But it will!' Mallory interrupted eagerly. 'Here's the letter from the textbook publisher. They're very interested.'

'Even so, I hardly have enough time to do my own work. Frankly, the idea of a book like this doesn't strike me as interesting at all.'

'No one's ever done it before.'

'Perhaps there's a reason for that.' He picked up his briefcase again.

Mallory found herself being urged gently towards the door. 'Won't you at least read it before you say no?' she pleaded, desperately. 'Or part of it, at least. It—it's a good book, and it would only take an hour.'

'First the girl demands two minutes, and then she wants an hour,' he mused.

Mallory grasped frantically for any idea that might keep him from walking away. 'If you don't have anything to do,' she said, 'I owe you a dinner. I kept you from eating last night——'

His eyebrows went up. 'Miss Mitchell, I would only have dinner with you tonight if you've reserved a table for fourteen, and we sit at opposite ends. Besides, I have plenty to do.'

'Oh. Well, then——'

'I'm not going to stand here in the hallway, Miss Mitchell. You can walk down to the parking lot with me if you like.'

'Generous of you.' It slipped out, and Mallory bit her tongue. When, she asked herself miserably, would she learn self-control?

His brown eyes gleamed with the first glint of humour she had seen him display. 'I only mentioned it because it would be very difficult to prevent you from tagging along,' he pointed out, and started down the stairs.

She fell into step beside him. 'There is a need for this book,' she said.

He showed no signs of hearing her. She rushed on, pessimistic, sure that nothing she could say now would make any difference, but determined not to give up as long as she had breath. He seemed to know that, and his stride lengthened until Mallory was taking two steps to his one, almost jogging in her effort to keep up with him.

He stopped abruptly beside a pale blue sports car, and she cannoned into him. Only her tight grasp on the manuscript kept it from flying out of her arms.

He unlocked the car and put his briefcase on the floor. Then he folded his arms along the top of the door and nodded at the manuscript. 'Is that the masterpiece?'

'No,' Mallory jeered. 'I always carry five hundred sheets of paper around with me. It's a marvellous exercise tool!'

He bit back a grin. 'Well, you're a good sport, I'll give you that,' he said. 'I suppose I'd feel like a fool if I turned down a chance to read what may be the best-selling textbook of next year.'

She looked from him to the stack of paper, uneasy about his sudden capitulation. 'You mean you actually want to read it?'

'Let's not stretch things,' he recommended. He reached for the bundle in her arms. 'Of course I don't *want* to read it, but I will. I make no guarantees about liking it, of course. But if I think it has value, I may be able to recommend someone for you to contact.'

Mallory wasn't quite sure she was hearing correctly. 'That would be super! And I promise not to pester you about it.'

'Very wise of you.' He got into the car.

'That is my only copy,' she called.

He rolled his window down. 'I'll be extremely careful with it,' he promised. The sports car's engine roared, and she retreated to the safety of the pavement as the car sped out of the car park.

The wave of relief that swept over her made her want to collapse on the concrete. It was the hardest day's work Mallory Mitchell had ever done.

Two weeks dragged by, and still she had not heard from him. Mallory was beginning to suspect that Dr Adams had no intention of reading her manuscript at all, that he had simply wanted to discourage her from bothering him about it any more.

That in itself would have been bad enough, she decided, but even worse was the fact that he possessed the only copy. If C. Duncan Adams damaged or destroyed that manuscript.... The very idea was enough to keep her tossing restlessly on her pillow in the long dark hours of the night, regretting the moment when she had promised not to call him about the book.

Her father was no help, either. Every time she mentioned it to him, he merely shrugged his shoulders and said that Duncan was a busy man. The delay didn't seem to bother him at all, and finally Mallory stopped talking to him about it altogether.

On the fifteenth day, Mallory could stand it no longer, and she stopped at Chandler College after finishing her day at the high school, intending to have it out with Dr Adams and at least recover her precious bundle. But his office door was locked. A sign on it, written in block letters in green ink and signed with an almost illegible scrawl, announced that he would not be holding regular office hours that day.

'What does he do, read minds?' Mallory muttered. 'It's as if he knew I was coming, so he ducked out!'

He has to show up some time, she thought. And if that meant that she had to drive over to campus every day to check on him, she would do it.

By the time she'd finished running her errands and got home, she was furious. The least the man could do was keep his promise, she fumed, or return her manuscript if he didn't intend to do anything with it!

She pulled into the driveway at a little faster speed than she usually did, and had to hit the brakes hard when she saw that Matt was playing one-on-one basketball with a friend in the driveway. She tapped the horn, and only then realised that the pale blue car which was parked on the street in front of the house was just like the one that Dr Adams drove.

No, she corrected herself automatically, as the two players looked up, and sunlight gleamed on one dark head and one blond. It was the same car.

And just why was C. Duncan Adams playing basketball in her driveway?

'Loose-limbed,' she muttered to herself, watching as he made a particularly graceful jump shot. 'I'd better look it up in Dad's dictionary—he must have a different edition than mine.'

'Hi, Mallory,' Matt called, and turned to his companion. 'See? I told you she'd be home soon.'

'Hello, Dr Adams,' she said quietly. 'I thought perhaps you'd gone off to New Guinea looking for a civilisation to study.'

'Oh, no. That would be anthropology—not my thing at all.'

She bit her tongue. I did tell him that I wouldn't ask about the book, she reminded herself. And, since he's here, that must mean that he's read it. I didn't exactly expect him to come here, though, she thought. I expected him to call and tell me I could pick it up at his office. At any rate, I'm not going to give him the satisfaction of asking him what he thought of it!

'What made you so late, Mallory?' Matt asked.

'It was my turn to babysit the kids who were making up time after school. Besides, didn't you hear Dad this morning? He told me he was having a craving for scallops, and would I please fix them for dinner tonight. I had to stop at the store.' No point in mentioning her side trip to the campus, she decided. She lifted a brown paper grocery bag out of the car.

Dr Adams moved quickly to her side. 'Let me help you with that.'

She almost dropped the bag in surprise before she recovered herself and surrendered it. So he was something of a gentleman, after all, was he? she thought.

He seemed to read her mind. 'It's self-defence,' he murmured. 'You can't drop it on my toe if I'm carrying it.'

She ignored the comment and held the back door for him. Her father must be home, she realised. There was a fresh pot of coffee on the kitchen counter. It was typical of the Professor to start the pot and then forget to come back and pour himself a cup. 'Would you like coffee?'

There was a twinkle in his eyes, but he said gravely, 'Yes, I would. If I can pour it myself.'

'I'm not usually as clumsy as I was that night at the dinner,' she snapped. She reached for a mug and handed it to him. 'I assure you that you're quite safe with me.'

'Of course,' he said, soothingly. He sat down at the table with his coffee, and watched as she unpacked the bag with brisk efficiency.

'I hope you don't mind if I start dinner while we talk,' she said over her shoulder.

'Why should I?' He looked at her curiously over the rim of his cup. 'Don't you ever relax, or is it just me? Are you always so touchy?'

She pulled her favourite cookbook off the shelf and started to turn the pages. 'You do seem to bring out the worst in me.'

'I'll try to be more careful,' he said sweetly. 'I would have thought with a teenage brother around you'd be accustomed to being teased.'

She started to bristle, and then saw the twinkle in his eyes. 'I'm going to take Dad his coffee,' she said. 'Make yourself comfortable, Dr Adams.'

'Thank you. My name is Duncan, by the way.'

Why was he being so friendly tonight? she wondered. Unless—it must mean that he had liked the book, that he intended to help her find someone to work on it!

Professor Mitchell was absorbed in his reading. Mallory set the cup down by his elbow and dropped a kiss on the top of his head. 'I think I have good news about the book,' she said.

'Oh?' He looked up quizzically, his eyes magnified by the half-lenses of his reading-glasses. 'Is Duncan here?'

'How did you know?'

'He told me yesterday that he might stop by.' He sipped his coffee. 'Why don't you invite him to stay to dinner, Mallory? Since it's scallops, and you do them so well——'

'Is that why you had the sudden craving this morning?' But her smile was fond. 'All right, if you want him, I'll ask. Shall I send him in to sit with you?'

'Oh, no, I'll see him at dinner.' The professor turned back to his book, and then looked up with a smile. 'That way I don't have to interrupt my work to talk to him,' he pointed out.

'I see. You're a selfish brute, Dad.'

Matt was coming down the stairs as she pulled the study door shut. 'Is Clyde staying for dinner?' he asked.

Mallory seized his arm. 'Don't you dare call him that!'

'All right, you've made your point. I promise. When's dinner?'

She glanced at her watch. 'Late, unless I start right now.'

Duncan Adams was standing at the sink, watching the birds who were squabbling over position at the feeder in the backyard. 'I never realised spring in the Midwest could be anything but dull and grey,' he mused.

'Where have you been all your life?' She propped the cookbook up on the counter. She could make this recipe from memory, and had, dozens of times. But she wasn't about to risk a failure tonight.

'West Coast. East Coast.' He shrugged. 'Just about every place.'

'That sounds marvellous.'

'What about you?'

'Right here. Dad started teaching at Chandler College the year I was born. I went up to the state university for a while, but when Mom died, I came home and finished college here, so I could help keep an eye on Matt. You're talking to a true product of middle America.'

'I'll remember that,' he said. 'It might come in handy in my research.'

She put a pot of water on to boil, and started to take ingredients out of the refrigerator. 'What are you doing here? Studying the natives?'

'Something like that.' He leaned against the sink, his arms folded. 'Curiosity is killing you, but you won't ask, will you?'

'Ask what?'

'You're dying to know what I thought of your book.'

She started to chop onions and garlic. 'And what did you think?'

'Do you believe I'm going to tell you while you're wielding that knife?'

She bit her lip. 'Oh. That bad?'

'Actually, I thought it was quite good.'

Mallory blinked, and looked up in shock.

'And I'd like to discuss it further, some time when I can have your full attention.'

The water came to a boil, and she added wild rice and stirred. 'How about after dinner? Dad wanted me to ask you to stay, anyway.' The memory of a disturbingly lovely blonde woman crossed her mind. 'If you can, that is.'

'What about you, Mallory? You're the one who gets stuck with the extra work.'

'Well, I'd certainly like to hear what you thought about the book. And it's really no effort to have a guest—I was going to do this, anyway.'

His smile was a thousand volts of pure charm, and Mallory felt slightly off balance. No wonder women of all ages so obviously found him attractive, she thought. That smile alone was enough to bring an unwary woman to her knees!

'In that case, is there anything I can do to help?' he asked.

'Yes,' she admitted, and smiled to take the sting out of what she was about to say. 'Stay out of my way. I'm an independent sort in the kitchen. Matt's in the family-room, I think——'

He laughed. 'I will take my marching orders with good grace.' He vanished down the hall, whistling.

He thinks the book is good! Mallory felt like bursting into song. And apparently, he didn't feel it necessary to check with Caroline before accepting a dinner invitation——

Though why Duncan Adams' domestic arrangements should make any difference to her was beyond Mallory's understanding. She turned back to the skillet where mushrooms were sautéing in butter, determined that this would be a dinner to remember.

Matt took one look at the dining-room table and said, 'Wow, Mallory! It's been ages since we've——'

A fierce look from his sister cut him off short. He stammered, and finished feebly, 'Had soup that looked so good.'

She looked down at the table, gleaming with crystal glassware, silver candlesticks, and her mother's best Irish linen tablecloth. Clear soup steamed gently from the four delicate china plates, and a bottle of wine was at her father's elbow. It had all looked so pretty a few minutes ago, when she had stood back and inspected her work. But now—now it seemed just a silly attempt to impress Duncan Adams. To show him that she wasn't a clumsy ox, after all.

She sneaked a quick look at him, under her lashes. Would he be embarrassed by all this? Or, what would be even worse, would he be amused by Matt's obvious surprise and the fact that she had gone to all this trouble?

To her relief, Duncan seemed not to have heard Matt's remark at all. He held Mallory's chair, and then seated himself next to her. 'This is astounding,' he said. 'Just a few minutes ago there was nothing going on in the kitchen, and now——'

Professor Mitchell laughed. 'Oh, Mallory's a wonder, that's sure! We're spoiled around here, Matt and I.' He expertly pulled the cork from the wine bottle and filled the glasses. 'To our guest,' he said.

Duncan smiled. 'A somewhat self-invited guest, I'm afraid.'

'Oh, we're delighted to have you, my boy.' The professor kept the conversation flowing through the soup, the scallops and rice, the crisp green salad. It had never ceased to amaze Mallory that a man who could be so horridly absent-minded as a guest at someone else's table was the world's best host.

And it was just as well, she thought, that no one was relying on her for small talk tonight. She'd been too busy with dinner preparation to think much about it before, but now her whole mind was on her book, and on what Duncan Adams would have to say about it after dinner. Had he really meant that he liked it? Had he thought of someone who might agree to be named as co-author of it?

Oh, how I will love writing back to the publishers, she thought, and telling them that the problem is solved! Perhaps in a week or two, the entire thing could actually be in the publisher's hands...

She pulled herself out of her dream. 'Matt, would you clear the table, please?' she asked. 'I'll bring dessert.'

When she carried in the tray of crystal plates, each bearing a large wedge of chocolate cake, she almost tripped over the small trolley where Matt had stacked the dishes. Her mother's china was haphazardly piled on the shelves.

I should have known better, Mallory thought. If we get out of this without a couple of pieces broken, it will be a miracle. But she bit her tongue and served the cake.

'Black Midnight cake,' Matt gloated, his fork poised above the fudge sauce that trickled over the puffy white frosting.

Professor Mitchell looked confused. 'But I thought you said this was to be a donation to the bake sale over at——'

'Yeah, Dad,' Matt said with relish. 'She threatened me with execution if I cut it.' He polished off his slice with a satisfied sigh. 'Boy, I'm glad you came to dinner, Duncan.'

She closed her eyes in pain. 'If you are quite finished, Matt,' she said firmly, 'I'm certain that you have homework to do.'

'That's the worst of having a sister who teaches at the same school,' Matt confided to Duncan. 'You can't get by with anything.'

Duncan laughed. 'After all that work, Mallory,' he said, 'surely you won't turn down an offer of help to clean up?'

Professor Mitchell cut in. 'Not necessary,' he said. 'Matt and I take turns in the kitchen. We're both hopeless at cooking, so we made a deal with Mallory. She feeds us—we clean up. Run along, now—I'll help Matt do the dishes.'

'It's your turn, Dad,' Matt said.

The professor shook his head. 'No. I don't forget things like that.'

Mallory ignored the squabble with an effort. 'Let's take our coffee to the living-room,' she said.

'I'll have to go and get your manuscript from the car.'

While she waited for him to return, Mallory got two mugs down from the kitchen shelf. Nothing fancy now, she thought—it was time to go to work, and her mother's delicate cups were just too dainty and small to be practical. She listened to Matt and her father, still wrangling over whose turn it was to do the dishes.

'Look,' she said, 'I don't care who does the work, but just be careful with the china, please. Make sure you have plenty of suds, and only put one piece in the sink at a time.'

Matt looked at her in horror. 'Do you mean this stuff can't go in the dishwasher?' he asked.

'That's exactly it. You break a piece, you die.'

'Wait till the PTA hears what a great cake it missed out on,' Matt muttered. 'And for such a reason...'

She gave up. 'Oh, dammit, Matt, leave the mess! I'll wash the china myself.'

'Children,' the professor interrupted. 'Mallory, get out of here. You're only making things worse by submitting to blackmail.'

Duncan was waiting for her, standing with his back to the arched doorway, running a gentle hand over the ivory keys of the grand piano. 'Do you play?' he asked when she came in.

'A little. My mother was the musician.' She set the tray down and closed the double doors that led to the hallway. Duncan raised an eyebrow, and she felt herself flushing a little. 'So we can concentrate,' she said, feeling foolish. 'Matt's being a little loud in the kitchen.'

He played a scale. 'The manuscript is over there,' he said, nodding towards the polished mahogany game table at the end of the room. 'I didn't expect to be impressed when I started to read it, but I was.'

It was more than she had dreamed of. Mallory swallowed hard. 'I'm glad you think it's good.' Hesitantly, she added, 'Did you find someone who will help me?'

He didn't answer. Another scale murmured through the room. 'Why did you write it?' he asked.

Mallory was confused. 'Well, because when I started teaching the class there weren't any materials, so I had to collect my own.'

'I know that,' he interrupted. 'It's in the preface. I mean, why did you write a book, instead of just giving lectures on the subject? Why was it so important to reach every student, not just those in your own class? And why did you take on a class like that, anyway? It's scarcely your field.'

Mallory's whole body stiffened. Her first instinct was to ask what business it was of his. Slowly, she forced herself to relax. Perhaps it *was* his business, she told herself. He was only trying to find out how serious she really was. He certainly wouldn't recommend that anyone devote time to helping her if she might give up the project at any moment.

'I'm very serious about finishing this book,' she said.

He looked up then. His eyes were unreadable, his face shuttered. 'That wasn't what I asked,' he said. 'If you don't want to tell me, that's your privilege, but——'

Mallory turned away. She stared out across the front lawn, where the street lights cast pools of cold light over the frosty grass.

He struck a minor chord, and turned from the piano. 'Good luck with the book,' he said. 'I'll let you know if I think of anyone who might be interested——'

'Wait!' She wheeled away from the window, took two fast steps, and almost collided with him. 'I'll tell you,' she said softly. 'It's just that it's hard to admit to a total stranger that you've made a very bad mistake in choosing a career——'

He smiled, slowly. It started in his eyes, which lit with a kind of golden glow. 'Once a person spills her dinner all over another person,' he pointed out gently, 'they stop being total strangers.'

Mallory's face flushed. 'Are you ever going to let me live that down?'

He didn't answer. Instead, he said softly, 'What sort of mistake did you make, Mallory?'

It was easier to say it if she wasn't looking at him. She fixed her eyes on a shirt button. 'I like teaching,' she said. 'And I love cooking and sewing and those things. So I assumed that I'd like to teach them. What I didn't realise is how little respect those classes get in the high schools. Students take them because they think it will be an easy grade. Counsellors push failing students towards them, to get the credits they need to graduate. Home economics is a poor relative——'

'And you feel cheated,' Duncan said perceptively.

'Yes.' She looked up then, and her eyes were bright with tears, brought there by his gentle voice. 'I'm a *good* teacher, and I feel as if I'm wasting my time——' She blotted her eyes.

'So you agreed to teach senior living. And you decided to do the best possible job of it.'

She nodded. It sounded so silly. She wasn't qualified. How on earth did she convince herself that she could handle such a thing? And then to write a book about it!

He was smiling again. She could hear it in his voice, even though she wouldn't look at him. 'I think I know someone who will help you,' he drawled. 'I've reconsidered, Mallory. I'm going to let you use my name as co-author.'

For a moment, she was so stunned she thought she hadn't heard him correctly. 'You?' she breathed.

'There are a few little things we'll need to work on, you understand——'

'Oh, of course,' she said eagerly. 'I'm just so delighted to have your backing that it took my breath away for a minute. Let's start right now, and perhaps over the weekend I can make the changes——' She pulled out a chair beside the game table, and riffled through the manuscript.

It looked a little battered with handling, no longer the pristine white pages with unmarred corners. It would all have to be retyped. Never again will I give anyone an original copy of anything she decided. Then she saw the first of the notes in the margins.

Green ink appeared on nearly every page. Sometimes it was a note off to the side, sometimes a word added or deleted, sometimes a circled number that led her to a slip of paper which had been inserted between her pages.

She looked up at him defiantly. '"A few little things"?' she said, her voice rising in anger. 'What in the hell have you done to my manuscript?'

'I've attempted to turn it into a book. Those are areas that require clarification, or further research, or——'

'You've rewritten the whole thing!'

Duncan shook his head. 'Oh, no. Not yet. What's the matter, Mallory? You don't sound quite so thrilled all of a sudden.' He pulled a sheaf of paper out of his pocket. 'Here's the plan for rewriting it.'

She was stunned into silence.

'It's up to you, of course,' he said cordially. 'You can keep going in this direction——' he gestured at the manuscript '—and end up with a wonderful monument to your ego, to store on the cupboard shelf. Or you can be professional about it——'

She slapped the first page of the manuscript as hard as she could. 'Tell me just where I was unprofessional. I did my research!'

He ignored her. '—and get it published. I'm not going to fight with you about it, Mallory. Which is it going to be?'

She stared at him, and then flipped through the pages of the manuscript, reading a green-inked note here and there.

I'm glad he didn't use red ink, she thought. The poor thing would look as if it had been wounded in combat. I'd like to just tell him to leave. What makes him think he knows so much? It's my book!

Yes, the other half of her mind reflected, and according to Dad he's written a whole shelf of them himself. He ought to know what's wrong with it.

So he thought it was a monument to her ego, did he? Well, she'd show him she could be as professional as anyone. Her book *would* be published——

But not without his help. That had been made amply clear by the publisher's letter. She had to have a co-author, and if it wasn't Duncan, she didn't know where to start looking.

'It's that bad?' she whispered, hardly knowing what she said.

'No. It's very good for an amateur, actually.'

Amateur! 'I've worked on this project for a year,' she protested.

'Then I'd say it would be foolish to give it up now.' His voice was flat, cool. He obviously didn't care, one way or the other.

She finally nodded. 'You're right.' She took a deep breath. Her heart was pounding, as if she was about to dive off the high board blindfolded. 'So—when do we start?'

# CHAPTER THREE

DUNCAN left at midnight with a sheaf of pages under his arm. Mallory said goodbye to him at the front door, and watched as he crossed the street to his car. She stifled a yawn as she turned the lights off in the living-room, leaving the manuscript scattered across the table. Her father's library was dark and silent, and the house creaked a little as she climbed the stairs.

Matt's bedside lamp was on, and his door was ajar. 'Well?' he asked in a stage whisper. 'Did Clyde kiss you goodnight?'

'Matt!' She stopped in the doorway. 'What a thing to ask! We're only working together.'

'What difference would that have made?' Matt asked airily. 'Did he?'

'Of course not. Go to sleep. You have school tomorrow.'

'So do you, but I notice it didn't keep you from entertaining Clyde till the wee hours.' Matt yawned enormously. 'And keeping me up, in the bargain.'

She was indignant. 'We were very quiet!'

Matt grinned evilly and punched his pillow into shape. 'I know. That's why I was worried about you.' He turned the light off with a snap.

Mallory undressed in the darkness of her room and crawled into bed. But, tired though she was, sleep didn't come easily. There were too many things to think about, too many exciting new possibilities offered by the events of the day.

\* \* \*

It was a very long week. Every evening Duncan appeared, immediately after dinner, with another rewritten section of the manuscript to return and another batch of research books to study. She had no idea where he was finding the time to do all the work; between her long days at school and the evenings spent with him, Mallory had discovered that the only time left for her own efforts in rewriting was late at night. The night before, she had fallen asleep at her desk after he'd left, and awakened in the cold hours of early morning to stagger to bed. She couldn't keep up this pace much longer, she was sure, but Duncan appeared to thrive on it. He certainly never looked tired!

On Saturday morning, she slept very late, and wandered downstairs barefoot and wearing a comfortably baggy old track suit. She would forget about the book today, she decided, and just enjoy herself. She deserved a day off, a little time to read and cook and relax. The only chore she really must do was to shop, but the rest of the day would be hers to do with as she pleased. And was she ever looking forward to it!

She ran into Matt in the hall. He had an apple in one hand and a half-eaten banana in the other.

'I was going to make coffee cake,' she said feebly.

'That's all right,' Matt told her with a superior air. 'Dad and I are learning to fend for ourselves these days. Randy Craig called, by the way.'

'He's Mr Craig to you, Matt.' What had Randy wanted? she wondered. 'Why didn't you yell at me?'

'Well, Clyde's been keeping you up till all hours. I thought you needed your sleep.'

'You're a love, Matt, but at all the wrong times.'

Matt raised an eyebrow. 'Oh? I had no idea you had it bad for Randy. He's a dishmop.'

'He is not. And I don't.'

Matt ignored her protest. 'And all this time I've thought it was Clyde. He's certainly been spending enough time here. Why don't you start charging him rent?'

'Matt, you don't need to be sarcastic. He's only here in the evenings, and then just to work.'

'Oh, really? Evenings only, hmmm? He's in the living-room right now, waiting for you. Maybe I should warn Randy that Clyde's trying to cut into his territory.' The back door slammed behind him before Mallory had gathered her poise.

Matt had been correct. She found Duncan bending over her work table, reading the half-finished page she had left in the typewriter, and she said sharply, 'Who let you in, anyway? And would you mind awfully if I finish a section before you start tearing it apart again?'

He finished reading the sentence before he turned. 'Oh, hello, Mallory.' He didn't sound upset at being caught. He didn't even sound in the least as if he felt guilty. 'You seem to be a little bad-tempered this morning. Aren't you getting enough sleep?'

'As if you cared!' Then, hating herself for even asking the question, she went on, 'What do you think of it?'

His eyes went to the page still in the typewriter. 'Actually,' he said, 'I think we should reconsider putting this bit in at all. I'm not convinced that it belongs in the book.'

For a moment, Mallory wasn't quite sure she'd heard him correctly. 'And just why do you think it should be left out?' she asked, her voice dangerously polite.

'It's got nothing to do with the subject, Mallory. The purpose of the book—you wrote it down yourself—is to help kids adjust to living on their own. Issues of parenthood really don't belong in that outline at all.' He tapped the chapter with an impatient finger. 'And the exercise you've used to illustrate this concept——'

Mallory interrupted. 'And just where have you been for the last ten years?' she snapped. 'For your information, kids this age are already making decisions about starting families, and they're choosing badly.'

'Granted, but——'

She ignored him. 'The issue is very simple—it's to help kids understand, using concrete examples, what a tremendous responsibility it is to have a baby. The hope is that once they understand that, they won't rush into parenthood in the belief that it would be wonderful to have this cuddly infant around. That's the only thing I'm trying to accomplish.'

'By using ordinary eggs as substitutes for babies?' he interrupted.

'Why not? They're suitable, they're inexpensive, they're available to anyone who wants to use the idea. It's not exactly original, Duncan. Teachers have been doing this for years. I'm just writing about how it's worked for me.'

He was looking at her as if he'd never quite seen her before. 'You're really hot about this, aren't you?'

'Yes, I am. Look, have you ever seen it done? The experiment with the eggs, I mean.'

'I'm glad you explained yourself,' Duncan murmured. 'I was beginning to wonder what on earth you thought I'd missed out on in my sheltered life...'

Mallory tried to fight down the colour that swept over her face. 'I wasn't asking if you knew where babies come from, that's sure! I only meant that if you don't know what you're talking about, how can you judge whether the idea is a success?'

'What do you recommend?'

'That you come to class a time or two and observe. I'll be handing out egg-babies on Monday, and the kids will be responsible for their care until the end of the school year. That's six weeks. Surely in that time you can fit in a visit or two?' She knew she sounded sarcastic, and she didn't care. If he was going to be a part of this project, he should at least be willing to devote some time to finding out what she was trying to accomplish!

He didn't seem to notice. 'Six weeks? Isn't that an awfully long time to invest in this experiment?'

'I've done this before, you know. It's not as if carrying an egg-baby around is the only thing they're doing for six weeks; the regular class work goes on. But this is the way it works best. At first, the kids think the eggs are just a game. About two weeks later they begin to think I'm being idiotic to insist on this. The last two weeks they begin to really think about the issues involved.'

'Who am I to quarrel with your egg-sperience?' Duncan murmured.

'Then you'll come to a class or two?'

'I'll try to fit it into my schedule.'

At least he'd made a partial concession, she decided. For the moment, that would have to be enough. 'In the meantime, I'll keep working on the section,' she said, wanting to make it clear that she had no intention of giving up on something she felt was so important.

'Stubborn, aren't you?' He didn't sound irritated, though. He might have been stating any sort of fact... Your hair is brown, your smile is charming, you look very sexy this morning——

These flights of fantasy have to stop, she told herself crossly. Duncan Adams had never said anything of the sort to her. A fleeting memory of a gorgeous blonde woman in a sparkly red dress nagged at the corner of her mind. With someone like Caroline around, she reminded herself, he wasn't likely to. She didn't quite understand why thoughts like this were bothering her, anyway. She certainly wasn't attracted to Duncan Adams herself. As far as she was concerned, Caroline was welcome to him. And if she could keep him at home once in a while, away from Mallory, that would be even better...

'I've almost finished rewriting the chapter on insurance, by the way.' She hesitated for an instant, and decided to tell him the truth; it never hurt to compliment a man, after all. 'You were right about it. It wasn't clear, and there just weren't enough examples. I think you'll like it now.'

The flattery seemed to glide over him without leaving a trace. 'When can I read it?'

'I should finish tonight.'

'On a Saturday night, you don't have anything better to do than write about insurance?' he asked.

'You seemed anxious to get it done.'

'I'm anxious, yes, but I'm not insisting that you spend every minute working.'

'Oh, really?' She knew she sounded a little nasty, and she didn't care. 'I can't think where I've gotten the impression that you were in such an awful hurry! Unless it's the fact that you've been haunting this house——'

'Well, it is only six weeks till the college term ends, you know, and I've already made plans for the summer.'

'A long vacation?'

He looked offended. 'Of course not! I have research to finish, and a book of my own to write.'

'I thought you said research is why you came here.'

He grinned. 'I make it a habit to study the natives, wherever I am. But a book can't be based on observation alone—you have to do the reading, as well.'

Did she read a hidden meaning into his tone? 'Was that a nasty crack about my book?'

'*Our* book, don't you mean, my dear?' His tone was silky. 'At any rate, I will be spending the summer in the library stacks at my Alma Mater and finishing up two years of work—so if our book isn't done by the middle of May...'

'I can take a hint.' After all, she thought, she was as anxious as he to have this done with.

'But, of course, I wouldn't want you to disappoint the man in your life by standing him up on a Saturday night.'

'I wouldn't dream of it,' she said sweetly.

'I'll stop by tomorrow and pick up that chapter.'

She stared at him, open-mouthed. First he told her to enjoy herself, then he insisted that the work be done by tomorrow! Just when did he think she was going to do it—between three and five in the morning? 'I'll call you when it's done!' she snapped.

But Duncan was already on his way to the door, and he didn't seem to hear.

She sighed, and went out to the little telephone nook in the hallway to call Randy Craig back.

'I've scarcely seen you all week,' he said. 'You haven't even been showing up in the cafeteria for lunch.' There was the hint of a question in his words, but Randy was too well mannered to come right out and ask what was going on.

It was just as well, Mallory thought. They might be dating, but he was still her boss, and if he had asked what she was up to, she would have had to tell him about the book. But she'd rather keep it to herself for as long as possible, and avoid any embarrassment in case the whole thing fell flat. Not even Duncan Adams' name, she reminded herself, was a guarantee of success, no matter what he seemed to think! 'I've been very busy,' she said, trying not to sound evasive. 'With midterm grades coming up, and all the class preparations to make every day——'

'I know you've got a heavy load,' he said. 'That's one of the things I wanted to talk to you about.'

Mallory's throat tightened. She hadn't meant to complain about the number of different classes she was teaching; it was a great deal of work, but she enjoyed the variety. 'What do you mean, Randy?'

'I've put my foot down and insisted that the social studies people take the independent living class off your hands next year,' he said.

'Randy, they don't want it——'

'They don't have a choice. You've done a wonderful job of organising that class, and now that you've proved it can be done, they no longer have an excuse for avoiding it. I've insisted that it be written into the new contracts that way.'

'But, Randy——' That's the one, of all of my classes, that I didn't want to sacrifice, she thought.

'Next year you'll have a little extra time,' he said, sounding very pleased with himself. 'At least you'll be able to have lunch every day.'

She tried to gather the words to protest, and couldn't. All the work of writing the book, and now it looked as if it would be for nothing! Someone else would teach her class, using her ideas and her plans.

'Are you busy tonight,' he asked, 'or would you like to go to a movie with me?'

She hesitated, but rebellion rose strong in her. Who cares? she thought. What difference does it make if the book is ever done? It won't be very useful if I'm not even teaching the class. She would work a while this afternoon, and if that wasn't enough to please Duncan, it would be just too bad. Besides, she could talk to Randy tonight, and tell him that she didn't want to stop teaching that class. She wasn't going to give up yet.

'I'd love to go to the movies,' she said, and thought, if Duncan wants that chapter done by tomorrow, he can just do it himself.

Though, she thought, she'd bet any amount of money that Duncan Adams wouldn't be spending his Saturday night sitting at home. She wondered where he would be, and with whom.

The grocery trolley she had grabbed at the supermarket's front door had a balky wheel, and no matter what Mallory did, the trolley wanted to run sideways down the aisle. She gritted her teeth and pushed harder, feeling like a trout swimming against the current.

The trolley took a sudden turn and collided with one that was parked carelessly in front of the cake mixes. 'I'm so sorry,' Mallory said breathlessly. Oh, no, she thought. Of all the luck! To run into Caroline, here!

The woman's smile had faded into a half-frown. 'Don't I know you?' she asked.

Mallory swallowed hard. 'Well, we weren't exactly introduced. I'm Mallory Mitchell.'

The woman's face cleared. 'Of course! You're Duncan's Mallory.'

Well, Mallory thought, that was certainly an unusual way to put it! Didn't Caroline mind all the time he was spending at the Mitchell house? Or did she perhaps not even know about it? Who was this woman, anyway?

'I'm Caroline Adams.' The blonde extended a slender hand. 'And I'm delighted to meet you. One of the women in the Newcomer's Club said I should talk to you.'

'Really?' Mallory asked, a little weakly. So Caroline was Duncan's wife, after all. She'd begun to think, because of all the free time he seemed to have, that he couldn't possibly be married...

And it makes not the slightest difference to you! she ordered herself crossly. Duncan Adams could have a half-dozen wives. But he doesn't wear a wedding ring, she thought, and was startled to discover that she had even noticed that small detail.

'Yes,' Caroline was saying. 'I've had so much trouble meeting people, you see. We've been here eight months now, and I still don't feel that I fit into the town very well.'

And just what, Mallory wondered, am I supposed to do about it? She would never have thought, from looking at Caroline Adams' slim figure, her perfect make-up, her elegant clothes, that this woman would have trouble making friends. There should be rafts of people hanging about her, waiting to be noticed. This was a small city, one in which a newcomer with Caroline Adams' kind of attractiveness would be instantly noticed.

'I should have thought the college community——' Mallory began.

Caroline shook her head. 'I don't fit in there at all, you see,' she said.

That's odd, Mallory thought. She remembered the shy but definite way that Caroline had declined to stay alone at the buffet dinner that night, when Duncan had said he was going home to change his sour-cream-soaked clothes. There was something very strange about this couple, she thought.

'Look,' Caroline said, 'can I buy you a cup of coffee or something? I'd really like to talk to you.'

Mallory glanced at her watch. 'Oh, I wish I had time,' she said insincerely. She saw Caroline's face close as if shutters had been slammed across her eyes.

I don't know why, Mallory thought, but this woman is desperately unhappy. I'm not thrilled that she chose me to reach out to, but I can't just turn my back on her. 'I'll make time,' she said firmly. 'I'd love a cup of coffee.'

In the next half-hour, Mallory found out more than she had ever wanted to know about Caroline Adams.

She knew that Caroline thought writing a book must be exciting, that she felt herself to be entirely without talent, and that her schedule as an evening-shift nurse at the local hospital left her without time for a social life.

'They've promised to move me to the day-shift next month,' Caroline said. 'So perhaps I can get involved in some activities. The people at the Newcomer's Club suggested I talk to you about the fund-raisers for the scholarship fund. It sounded like fun.'

'I'm in charge of them,' Mallory admitted. 'But most of the parties are over for the year, and the schedule is set for next season.' Her regret was sincere; she had had to twist arms to get people to host parties with the proceeds from ticket sales benefiting the college. To have a volunteer appear, too late, was heartbreaking.

'Oh, I don't want to give a party.' Caroline sounded panicky. 'But I thought there might be things I could help with. I can do paperwork, or serve meals——'

'You're the kind of volunteer I'd give my right arm for,' Mallory said. 'You've got a job, my dear. Why don't you come to tea tomorrow and we'll talk about it?'

'Oh, I couldn't! I wouldn't want to intrude——'

'We hold open house every Sunday. I never know who is coming, or how many, but I think you'll find some interesting people. Four o'clock, at Seventeen Armitage Road.'

She didn't wait for an answer. It would be interesting, she thought, to see if Caroline showed up.

They were at the cinema early that night. Randy was always punctual. He made a joke of it as they watched the rows of seats fill around them. 'It's a compulsion, I suppose,' he explained, 'but, since I was a kid, I never felt I got my money's worth at the movies unless I saw all the previews, too. My ex was always late. It was one of the things we fought about all the time.'

Mallory shifted uncomfortably in her chair. She didn't like it when Randy talked about his marriage; she always felt that she was being compared to his ex-wife and, even when it was favourable, it made her nervous.

He looked down at his popcorn box. 'Of course, being early has its drawbacks. I always eat twice as much popcorn as anyone else. Would you like more?'

'No thanks,' Mallory said with a smile. 'I wouldn't want you to be standing in line at the confectionery stand when the main feature starts.'

He grinned. 'Any more smart remarks from you, and I won't take you for pizza after the show.'

'I'll be very good,' she promised solemnly.

Randy discarded the empty popcorn box and looked around. 'It must be a good movie,' he observed. 'There's certainly a crowd tonight. Half of the high school is here.'

'You don't really believe they came to watch the show, do you?'

Randy smiled. 'Come to think of it, probably not.' His eyes focused suddenly on the third row in front of them. 'That,' he said, 'is the most beautiful woman I've ever seen.'

Mallory had never heard quite that tone in his voice before. She followed the direction of his gaze, and understood. The lights in the cinema died just as Caroline Adams turned her classic profile back towards the screen.

Mallory had seen her for just a split-second, then suddenly the auditorium was too dark for her to see if Duncan was there, too. She supposed he must be, though. Caroline wasn't the type to go to the cinema alone.

'Very nice,' she said, keeping her voice level.

Randy looked at her quizzically in the light that reflected from the screen. 'Sorry,' he said. 'That wasn't very tactful, was it? My ex and I used to fight about that, too. But I really didn't mean it as it sounded. I'd have said the same thing about a painting, or a statue——'

'Don't miss any of the movie,' Mallory recommended, and he subsided.

The film was a musical extravaganza, all glitter and sparkle and sharp production numbers. The storyline required little attention to follow, which was fortunate for Mallory. She would have had trouble keeping track of the plot of a cartoon.

Why, she asked herself, should she have felt that stab of jealousy at the very sight of Caroline Adams? Randy hadn't done anything out of the ordinary; he hadn't been exaggerating when he said his reaction would probably have been the same to a piece of art as it had been to this first glimpse of that gorgeous woman. So why should Mallory have gone suddenly green?

It wasn't as if she and Randy were engaged. They were friends, that was all. Or was it more than that? Had she come to care for Randy Craig, so slowly that she hadn't even known herself what was happening?

She was still thinking about it when the film was over. She was half-blinded when the lights came up, and she stumbled and grabbed for Randy's arm on the way up the aisle. There was a bottleneck at the doors, and they stood in line for a few moments, waiting to reach the exit.

Then a voice reached out to her. 'Mallory, I didn't see you earlier.'

She turned, easily. She'd been expecting it, after all. 'Hello, Caroline.'

Out of the corner of her eye, she could see the stunned expression on Randy's face. He seemed to be saying, accusingly, 'You know her, and you didn't offer to introduce me?'

'Is Duncan with you?' Mallory asked. Tactless as it was to ask, she suddenly had to know.

'Yes. But he stopped to speak to a student. I didn't want to hold up traffic, so I walked on.' Caroline gave a nervous little laugh. Her eyelashes fluttered as she glanced up at Randy.

The thing that is so hard to believe, Mallory told herself, is that she doesn't even know she's flirting. I'd swear that she doesn't know it! 'Caroline, this is my friend——'

'Randall Craig,' he supplied eagerly, a hand outstretched to clasp Caroline's. 'And you are——'

'Caroline Adams,' she said, very softly.

And I am totally unnecessary, Mallory told herself.

'We were just going to have a pizza,' Randy volunteered. 'If you'd like to join us——'

'I don't know.' Caroline turned. 'Duncan, we've been invited to join Mallory and Mr Craig——'

'Call me Randy, please,' he begged.

'Randy, then,' she repeated softly. 'Would you like to have a pizza, Duncan?'

Duncan put his arm around Caroline's shoulders. 'Whatever you'd like to do, my dear.'

Mallory watched as comprehension dawned on Randy's face. He looked miserable. It served him right, she thought vindictively. He should have expected that there would be competition at hand, with a woman as attractive as Caroline Adams!

'Oh,' Caroline stammered. 'I forgot to introduce you. Mallory, of course you already know Duncan. Randy, this is Duncan——'

Mallory looked up at Randy through dark eyelashes, not wanting to miss the look on his face when he discovered that his newly discovered piece of art was a married woman.

'My brother,' Caroline finished. 'And we'd very much like to join you and Mallory for a pizza.'

# CHAPTER FOUR

IF A sledgehammer had suddenly descended on Mallory's head, it wouldn't have stunned her quite as much as Caroline's soft announcement did.

But she as much as told me they were married! Mallory found herself thinking frantically.

She realised belatedly that she was being observed. Duncan was watching her, one eyebrow quirked, his coffee-coloured eyes inquisitive. Of course, she thought. Why didn't I realise how much they resemble each other? Duncan's odd combination of blond hair and brown eyes—Caroline had it, too. She glanced around. Randy and Caroline had disappeared.

'They went on ahead,' Duncan murmured. 'Caroline's riding with your friend. You're supposed to come with me, to help me find my way to the Pizza Palace.'

'You can't get there by yourself?'

'There's no need to be sarcastic,' he protested mildly. 'As a matter of fact, I'm reasonably sure I can find the way. But your friend seemed very concerned about me. He didn't think I should be left on my own.'

Mallory said, 'He's very attracted to Caroline.' She was proud of herself; her voice was perfectly steady, and her tone was almost amused.

'Are you jealous?' Duncan murmured. He held the door for her. 'My car is just up the street.'

'Jealous?' Mallory shivered in the crisp breeze and pulled the hood of her coat closer around her face. The fur trim tickled her cheek. She would be so glad, she thought, when the last of winter finally disappeared, and spring stopped playing hide-and-seek and settled in to stay. 'Of course I'm not jealous.' She was uneasily aware that it wasn't quite the truth, but she certainly wasn't going to tell Duncan about that odd twinge! 'Whatever gave you such an idea?'

'The fact that you've turned emerald-green around the edges.'

'You're imagining things.'

'Well, let me give you a warning. Standing there with smoke coming out of your ears while your boyfriend ogles another woman is no way to make your point with him, that's sure.' They reached the little blue sports car, and he pulled out his keys. 'There are many more effective ways of dealing with the situation.'

'I told you, I'm not jealous.'

'I heard you. I don't believe you.' They were half-way to the Pizza Palace before he spoke again. 'I'll bet that by the time he takes you home you'll tear into him——'

Mallory had been staring out of the window. 'And what business is it of yours if I do?' She sighed. 'Are you doing research on dating behaviour now? Or are you concerned about Caroline? She's perfectly safe with him. Randy's a gentleman——'

'Some gentleman. Ditches his date when a——' He broke off abruptly.

'Don't mind my feelings,' Mallory said crisply. 'When a prettier girl comes along, is that what you were going to say?'

Duncan chuckled. 'That wasn't exactly it, but it'll do.'

'Thanks a lot.'

'My point is that there are a lot better ways of responding to it than you're doing at the moment. You're feeling inadequate; that's only natural. He gave you a bit of a jolt. But if you show him that's how you feel, you'll only be encouraging him to think that you're not worth worrying about.'

'So what do you recommend, Dr Adams? You're the expert.'

'Hmm. I'll work on it.'

'Well, work fast. There's the Pizza Palace, and they've already arrived.' Mallory's voice was heavy with sarcasm. As if she needed his help, or advice!

Duncan parked his car next to Randy's, directly under one of the brilliant lamps that lit the car park. 'Sit still,' he said. 'I'll come around and open your door.'

'I can do it by myself,' she snapped, but he had already got out of the car. By the time she had pushed the door open, he was waiting. He took her hand to help her out of the car, and then said, on a note of discovery, 'I've got it. It's very simple, really.'

'I can't wait to hear this,' Mallory said.

'You need to give him something to be jealous of, in return.'

'That's childish.'

'But it works. Let me show you.'

'Thanks for the thought,' Mallory said quickly, 'but I'd really rather——'

He didn't seem to hear, and there was no place for her to run. She was trapped in the narrow triangle formed by the car, the open door, and his body. She put her hand against his chest and pushed, but it was like shoving against a rock wall.

His gloved hand rested on her cheek for an instant, the leather cold against her skin. Then his fingers worked slowly under her hood to the nape of her neck and drew her close.

Duncan's lips were cold against hers, but the sensation that rocked her was of liquid fire pouring through her body. She started to tremble violently, as though a fever held her in its grasp. Her hood slipped off her head, and dark hair spilled over the fur trim.

'I'm so sorry,' he said, when he finally raised his head. 'I've mussed up your hair.'

'On purpose,' Mallory retorted. She tried to restore a little order to the mess, and finally gave up, pulling the few remaining pins out and shaking her head to let the waves fall into place.

Duncan smiled. 'You don't expect me to admit that, do you? I was overcome by your charms——'

'No one would believe that for a minute.'

'Certainly not if you go in looking like a thundercloud.'

'I'll deal with Randy in my own way, Duncan. I don't need your help!'

'Too late,' he said comfortably.

'What do you mean?'

'He and Caroline are sitting in the booth by the window. Your precious Randy saw the whole thing.'

'Why, you——' She twisted around to look, and realised that he was not exaggerating. Through the tinted glass of the restaurant window, Randy was staring at her.

'We'd better get you inside before you freeze,' Duncan added. Solicitously, he pulled her hood back up around her face, holding it close with both hands while he smiled down into her eyes. Mallory wanted to kick him.

He followed her into the restaurant, making no effort to touch her in any way. At first, she was relieved. Then she realised that to an observer, it might have been less suspicious if he had been holding her hand! This way, it must look as if they had plenty to hide.

Caroline and Randy were sitting side by side in the booth. Mallory slid on to the bench opposite them and planted her handbag firmly beside her on the seat, where it would be between herself and Duncan. Just as firmly, he picked it up, reached across her, and set it on the windowsill.

'Have you ordered?' he asked the couple across the table.

'No,' Randy said. 'We've only been here a couple of minutes.'

'That's good,' Duncan said expansively. 'We were afraid we'd be late. We were held up by...mmm... traffic.'

Randy looked bemused by the blithe contradiction of what he had seen happening in the car park. Mallory kicked Duncan's ankle under the table. He looked down at her with a raised eyebrow and retaliated, inching closer to her, until the length of his thigh was pressing against hers. The contact was like lightning flickering along her veins, but it didn't seem to concern Duncan. He simply carried on a normal, chatty conversation, as if completely unaware of the trauma he was causing her. And every time Mallory moved a fraction of an inch, he casually shifted his position until he had restored that hidden contact, an intimate secret between the two of them, concealed from the others at the table.

Eventually Mallory found herself wedged into the corner of the booth, with no place left to run to, so she bit her tongue and decided to sit still and make the best of it, rather than sacrificing her dignity by asking him to move over. And as soon as she was alone with him, she decided, she would waste no time in making herself clear. She certainly hadn't asked him to do this; *she* wasn't the one who had decided that Randy needed straightening out!

They talked, ate pizza, drank beer, and talked some more. Randy and Duncan did most of the talking; Caroline was too shy, and Mallory too conscious of Duncan beside her to pay much attention to what they were saying. She was relieved when Duncan smiled down at her and said, 'It's getting late, and the manager keeps looking over at us, as if he'd appreciate it if we got out of here and let him close the doors.'

He'll get no argument from me about going home, she thought, and began to frame in her mind the cold and cutting words she would use to put him in his place. He'd never dare to interfere in her life again, after she got through with him tonight...

Duncan went on. 'Are you ready to go, Caroline?' It wasn't really a question, and Caroline wordlessly began to gather up her jacket, scarf, and handbag.

Mallory's mouth dropped open. Surely she had heard wrong!

Randy made a feeble half-protest, to the effect that he'd be happy to see Caroline home.

Duncan cut it off in the middle, with a smile. 'Now that would be a little silly, don't you think?' he said gently. 'We live all the way across town. In any case, I've always made it a point to personally see that the lady I started the evening with gets home.'

Randy turned bright red.

'I'll see you tomorrow, Mallory,' Duncan added quietly.

They were gone before Mallory had found her voice. 'Well!' she said finally.

Randy was staring at her across the table. 'You were ready to ditch me, weren't you?'

The accusation stung, all the more so because it was true. 'You're the one who offered to drive Caroline home,' Mallory pointed out.

'Well, at least I wasn't kissing her in the car park!'

She was furious. 'Only because you weren't offered the opportunity!' she retorted.

'You certainly didn't hesitate when you were offered the chance to find out what Mr Wonderful can do!'

The reproach hurt, and Mallory struck back, with sweet sarcasm in her voice. 'Randy, why are you so certain that was the first time I've kissed him? Are you jealous?' No sooner were the words said than she regretted losing her temper. After all, she was in no position to be throwing stones. She tried to patch it up. 'We've never actually said we wouldn't date other people, you know——'

He didn't seem to hear the half-apology. 'I suppose that's what you've been so busy with all week,' he said brusquely. 'Get your coat on, Mallory.'

He drove her home in silence and didn't even turn the engine off at her front door.

'Thanks for the movie,' she said.

He nodded coldly and drove off.

She went straight to her desk. She hadn't missed the hidden meaning in Duncan's farewell. 'I'll see you tomorrow,' he had said, meaning that he'd come by to pick up the chapter she had promised. She rolled a sheet of paper into the typewriter and turned over a page of notes, trying to frame a sentence in her mind.

But all she could see was Duncan's eyes as he had bent his head to kiss her. Coffee-coloured eyes, that had been very dark right then in the yellowish light from the car park lamps. Coffee-coloured eyes, and a mouth that was cold to the touch, but which had sent the hot blood pounding in her ears...

She turned the typewriter off and went to bed. If Duncan Adams wanted her to work on this book, she decided, he was going to have to learn to keep his hands off her personal life!

A pan of scones was browning nicely in the oven, under Mallory's watchful eye, when Melinda knocked on the back door. 'Do I smell chocolate cake?' she asked. 'I was hoping that you hadn't gotten so busy that you'd given up the tradition of Sunday tea.' She was dressed in jeans and a sweater, and her hair was in pigtails; her students at the high school would not have recognised her as the maths teacher they were used to.

'You haven't come to tea in ages.'

'That's true, but I thought perhaps if I came over here, I could talk to you.' She settled herself at the kitchen table. 'I've hardly seen you for days. And all week, Randy Craig's been asking what happened to you.'

Mallory sighed. 'Not any more he isn't.'

Melinda looked intrigued. Before she could question, though, Professor Mitchell came in. 'Are you expecting a crowd today, Mallory?' he asked hopefully. 'If you're not, I thought perhaps I'd just take my tea into my office and work on my lecture series. I have that big tour set up for summer, you know, and——'

Mallory cut him off. 'Sorry, Dad,' she said. 'It's not a crowd, actually, but there are a couple of people that I was depending on you to entertain.'

'Oh? Someone new?'

'Yes. Duncan's sister is supposed to drop in, and since she doesn't know any of our regulars I'm afraid she might not be too comfortable. If you could take care of her, introduce her around——'

The professor looked less than pleased. 'I can't imagine Caroline Adams needing a nursemaid at a tea party.'

Mallory stopped dead, her knife poised above the stack of sandwiches, and said, before she had a chance to think about it, 'You knew who she was, and you didn't tell me?'

The professor's eyebrows elevated. 'Why should I? You never asked, and there was scarcely time for an introduction at the banquet.'

Mallory cut the sandwiches with unnecessary force.

'Besides,' he went on, 'I don't know her all that well—just who she is.' He grumbled around the kitchen a bit, and then, when Mallory showed no further inclination to listen to him, retreated to the living-room where the tea table was already set up.

Melinda kept a straight face till he was gone. 'Every time I'm here,' she said, 'your father has an excuse for missing tea. And every time he mentions it, you give him a reason that means he has to show up. And the reasons are always different! Where do you find them all, Mallory?'

Mallory shrugged. 'It's easy, really. He makes a fuss about it, but his manners are too good for him to argue with me. Besides, I think he really enjoys having people in to tea.'

'He hides it very well,' Melinda said drily. 'Now, you were talking about this Duncan. Who's Duncan?'

'Why do you ask?'

'Because the way you and the professor were talking about him just now, he sounds like a member of the family, that's why. And I've never heard his name before. Is Duncan his first name or his last?'

'Middle.' Mallory scooped the evenly browned scones off the pan and on to a delicate china plate lined with a fragile lace doily. 'He's C. Duncan Adams and he's a colleague of Dad's at the college. That's all.'

Melinda raised an eyebrow. 'It certainly doesn't sound as if that's all,' she murmured. 'Fury is seeping from your every pore. What's the "C" stand for, anyway?'

'I don't know.' Then Mallory, remembering the casual way he had interfered in her life, as if he had the right, tossed caution to the winds. She had to say something, or explode! 'My suspicion is that it's short for *conniving*. Or possibly *cunning*. Or——'

'I'm hurt,' said a voice from the doorway. 'After last night, I was certain you'd think I was *captivating*. You must admit I was at least *congenial*——'

'On the other hand,' Mallory said to Melinda, ignoring the man lounging in the doorway, 'it may just stand for *Casanova*. Watch yourself.'

'Oh, I shall,' Melinda said sweetly. She was eyeing Duncan, discreetly. 'This is Duncan? He doesn't look like a colleague of your father's.'

Mallory was not going to try to explain. 'Would you mind if I asked you to leave, Melinda? I need to talk to Duncan for a minute.'

'Of course I don't mind. Shall I take the scones in?' She picked up the plate and paused beside Duncan in the doorway. 'Mallory and I never poach each other's territory,' she murmured. 'We've been friends for far too long. But if you ever decide to change camps, I'm in the phone book. Melinda Anderson.' She slipped past him and vanished across the hall.

'Tea is in the living-room,' Mallory pointed out.

'I didn't come for tea. I came to see you.'

Simple words, and absolutely accurate, she thought. There was no reason why her heart should have made that funny little leap clear up into her throat. He meant that he had come for the completed chapter, that was all. The episode last night had been only an isolated incident, not part of anything that would continue. And thank heaven for that, she told herself.

'I'm not finished,' she announced. She started to wipe up the counter where she had rolled the scones out to cut them into fancy shapes.

'I'll help,' he said. 'I'm an expert at cleaning up messes in the kitchen. I make so many of them, you see.'

'I wasn't talking about this. I meant that I'm not finished with the chapter.'

'I'm not surprised.' He sounded very calm.

'Do you mean that you're not angry about it?'

'Should I be?'

'You seemed in such a hurry——'

'I mean that I understand. Aren't you ever alone around here? There's always a party going on, or a meal to fix, or someone wanting to talk to you. When do you ever have time for yourself, Mallory?'

Incredibly, he sounded gentle, as if he really cared. She swallowed a lump in her throat. 'After Matt's in college, I suppose. It's only two more years. And as for the rest—the parties and all—I do that because I like it.'

'I see.' There was a long silence. 'Is that what you wanted to talk to me about?'

No, she thought. I was going to tell you not to ever dare to touch me again, and I was going to explain to you the results of your little game last night.

But now it seemed merely silly. He certainly wasn't having any trouble keeping his hands off her today, and what point was there in detailing her quarrel with Randy? He would probably be amused by both of her concerns.

She finished wiping off the counter and rinsed her dish-cloth. 'Shall we go and have tea?' she asked, finally. It seemed to her that there wasn't enough air in the kitchen to breathe any more, that if she had to stay there alone with him she would suffocate. Already, she was feeling just a little dizzy.

Duncan looked down at her for a moment, and smiled as if he was reading her mind. 'Is that what you really want to do?' she asked, very softly.

'Yes.' Mallory kept her voice firm, and tried to ignore the way his eyes crinkled at the corners with amusement. She turned towards the living-room and pushed away the tiny flicker of regret that he hadn't stopped her.

Melinda was perched on the edge of the couch, behind the massive tea service, spreading whipped cream on to a scone with a connoisseur's enjoyment, making certain that every crumb of the surface was covered. 'The best part of a scone,' she said, admiring her handiwork, 'is the fantastic weight of strawberry jam and whipped cream that it can support.' She popped the morsel into her mouth and chewed with evident enjoyment. 'Mallory makes her own strawberry jam, you know,' she told Duncan.

'I'm not surprised.'

'I didn't think you'd mind if I poured,' Melinda went on, smoothly, 'since I had no idea how long you'd be...occupied. One lump, Mallory?'

'Please.' She ignored the speculative tone in Melinda's voice. 'And I certainly don't mind if someone besides me pours the tea. It's nice to have help.' She stirred her tea, sat down with a sigh in her favourite chair, and looked around the room.

Caroline and Professor Mitchell were at the far end of the room. They seemed to be reading the titles on the bookshelves that surrounded the fireplace. Mallory thought it looked a little odd as a pastime, but if it was the sort of thing that kept Caroline happy, who was she to question it?

The doorbell rang. She glanced down the room at her father, whose job it was to answer it, but he hadn't seemed to hear. She set her cup and saucer aside with a sigh.

Randy Craig was on the doorstep. 'I'm sorry,' he said. 'I was an idiot last night, and if you never want to speak to me again, I deserve it.'

'I wasn't exactly on my best behaviour last night, either,' she said. 'Let's just forget it, shall we? Come in and have tea with us.'

'Who's here?'

Mallory sighed. 'Caroline, for one,' she said, thinking that it would probably be best to warn him. 'And Duncan.'

Randy seemed to freeze, just a little. 'I see,' he said.

Mallory began to regret the day that she had decided not to tell Randy about her book. Randy, Melinda, maybe even Caroline—they had all decided that her association with Duncan was a romantic one. Maybe I should take out an ad in the local newspaper, she thought, and announce that we're only writing a book, for crying out loud!

When they went in, Caroline came across the living-room with a smile, her hands outstretched. Today she was wearing a tailored suit in soft blue, with a tiny matching hat, and she looked fantastic. Mallory sneaked a look up at Randy, who appeared to be both startled and pleased at this reception. But Caroline came directly to Mallory. It was as though she hadn't seen Randy at all.

'Mallory, my dear,' she said, 'I'm sorry I didn't see you come in a few minutes ago. It was dreadful of me not even to say hello to my hostess! But I was so absorbed in what Hal was telling me about your cabinet full of little animals——' She glanced up at Professor Mitchell, beside her, with a smile.

Hal? Mallory thought. In her twenty-four years, she had never heard Professor Harold Mitchell referred to as Hal.

'He said you've been collecting pairs for years,' Caroline went on.

Mallory said, absently, 'Since I was very young. I've always liked tiny things, and so my mother started bringing me pairs of baby animals made out of all sorts of materials.'

'Hal said you have even more upstairs. I'd love to see them all some day. I've just remembered—Duncan, do you know where I put that pair of blown glass lovebirds that you brought me from Venice years ago? I don't think

I've seen them since we moved, but I'll look for them. I'd like you to have them, Mallory.'

'Oh, I couldn't. You wouldn't want to give something like that away.' And I wouldn't want them, she added to herself. Lovebirds that Duncan had brought home?

Caroline smiled. 'But of course I'm serious, dear. I just have them wrapped up in tissue somewhere, in a box. You would put them out where they could be enjoyed.' She looked up at Professor Mitchell, and put a slender hand on his sleeve.

My God, Mallory thought, she really is flirting with my father! Randy was beginning to look a little frayed around the edges. Apparently he had conveniently forgotten his earlier decision not to make a fool of himself over Caroline again.

'You must be very proud of her,' Caroline told the professor. 'I know Duncan is.'

That got Randy's attention. He shot a questioning look at Mallory, who concealed a sigh and sat down in the closest chair. 'I'm getting too old for this,' she muttered under her breath.

Only Melinda heard her. She filled a teacup and handed it to Randy. 'Go sit down,' she ordered him. 'You look like a fish, opening and closing your mouth in shock like that.

He did so, obediently, as if stunned that someone in Melinda's position would have the nerve to tell him what to do.

Duncan, who had been an interested spectator from his corner, came over to have his cup refilled, and then perched on the arm of Mallory's chair.

She shifted nervously away from him. 'Don't make it worse,' she hissed. 'Go away, would you, please?'

'But I have a much better view from here,' he protested.

'Well, I don't.'

'Oh, that's all right. I'll give you a running commentary.'

'That I do not need. Please, Duncan——'

He merely slanted an amused look down at her, and casually arranged his arm across the back of her chair, so the tweed sleeve of his jacket brushed against the nape of her neck. It reminded her of the sensation his leather glove had produced in that very spot the night before, and she shivered.

'Where is Matt today?' he asked. 'I didn't think he'd miss food.'

'He's visiting his girlfriend.' How could he be so casual? she wondered. The touch of his sleeve was driving her crazy.

The ringing of the doorbell was like a release from prison. She jumped up from her chair before the professor could make a move towards the front hall, admitted the newcomers, murmured to Melinda that she believed another batch of scones would be needed, and retreated to the kitchen, hoping that no one would miss her.

It was, of course, a futile hope. She was just patting the dough out into a rectangle when Duncan appeared. She sighed and began cutting out shapes with far more force than was necessary. 'If you're still trying to make Randy jealous,' she began, 'you obviously haven't noticed what a hopeless project it is.'

'But just as obviously, you have. Have you given up on him, then?'

'I'm not dumb.' She slid the scones on to a baking sheet. 'And I'm not heartbroken over it.' Even if it wasn't quite true now, she told herself, then it would be some day. She would work very hard at getting over Randy; if he was going to pursue Caroline, Mallory didn't want to make a fool of herself. 'Caroline's got no competition from me.'

'You're saying that you really don't care?'

'Oh, well, my pride is hurt, but apart from that——'

He murmured something that she didn't quite catch, and came to stand behind her. She hoped that he would interpret her flushed cheeks as the result of the hot oven.

'Randy wouldn't be happy with Caroline for very long,' he said, thoughtfully. 'And I don't think Caroline would be happy with him.'

'Don't you think that they are the ones who must decide that?' She found that she was having just a little trouble breathing; the warmth of his chest was pressing against her spine, and his hands were carelessly massaging her upper arms, as if he was absorbed in his thoughts and unaware of what he was doing. 'Besides,' she whispered, 'I think that's a dreadful thing to say about your sister.'

His eyebrows arched. 'I wasn't slicing up her character,' he denied. 'I was stating a fact.'

'Still——' She tried to swallow the lump in her throat, and said, 'Besides, it's scarcely flattering of you to push him at me just because you don't think he's suitable for your sister.'

'Why not? You had him first.' Before she could argue the point, he said, 'How far did you get with that chapter, by the way?'

The sudden shift startled her as much as if the floor had suddenly caved in under her feet. 'I told you it wasn't finished.'

'I know. I just wondered how much progress you'd made.'

'Not much,' she confessed. 'There were too many other things——'

'That's what I thought.' He released her abruptly. 'We're going to have to do something about that.'

Mallory sighed. 'Don't ask the impossible, Duncan. You know how hard I worked all last week. I've only taken the weekend off, for heaven's sake——' She felt cold, suddenly, in the presence of this abruptly professional man. What was he going to demand next?

'We'll have to do something, Mallory, or we aren't going to complete the book before summer comes.'

She said, unhappily, 'We could finish when you come back in the fall.' But she knew that the long delay would risk the whole project. By then, the publisher might have lost interest altogether.

He was staring out of the window, and he didn't seem to hear what she had said. Then, abruptly, he turned and left the room.

Mallory sagged against the sink in relief. Just being in a room with Duncan was a wearing experience, she thought. She didn't see him again. By the time the scones were done, another group had appeared for tea, and Duncan and Caroline had gone. Mallory told herself that she was relieved.

Her father helped to tidy up the mess after the last of their guests had departed. Mallory rinsed a crystal dish, put it on a towel to drain, and said, 'I'm sorry Caroline attached herself so thoroughly to you. I didn't quite expect that she would take up your whole afternoon.'

He looked up from the cups and saucers he was loading into the dishwasher, his eyes bright. 'Don't worry, Mallory. I didn't take it seriously.'

'Dad! That's not what I meant——'

'Be honest, dear. Weren't you concerned that an old man like me might misinterpret the lady's actions?'

'Well, whenever I paid any attention, she seemed to be flirting with you,' Mallory said uncomfortably. 'Calling you Hal, for heaven's sake——'

'Don't fret. It's been a long time since a lovely woman trifled with me. I rather enjoyed it.' He sighed theatrically, and put his hand over his heart. 'She can practise on me any time she likes.'

She laughed. 'Personally,' she said, 'I don't blame Caroline. I think you'd be a lot of fun to flirt with. You know the rules, which is more than most men do.'

The professor pursed his lips thoughtfully. 'Does that mean you haven't been very successful lately? I noticed that Randy seems to have gone overboard.'

Mallory looked at him in astonishment. So that preoccupied look and those sleepy eyes of his were false, were they? 'You don't miss a trick, do you, Professor?'

'That, my dear, didn't take much intuition. He stared at Caroline all afternoon. Or were you referring to Duncan? Though I can't imagine him not knowing the rules. He might not always obey them——'

'Oh, Duncan knows how to play the game, that's sure.' She caught herself too late. There had been a tinge of bitterness in her words.

The professor didn't question her. 'The book will eventually be completed, and then you won't have to see him any more,' he said, soothingly.

I know, Mallory thought, and that's the problem.

She caught herself up short. What on earth was she thinking about? Where had that stray idea come from— the notion that she might miss Duncan Adams once this project was finished?

What utter nonsense, she told herself briskly.

'He seems to be pitching right in to help with the book,' the professor added.

'Oh, he's involved, all right.' She climbed on to a stool and started putting the tea things away in the highest cupboard.

'Above and beyond the call of duty, I'd say.' Her father handed the teapot up to her. 'Though I must admit I was surprised at you letting him take the manuscript home today.'

She reached for the tea strainer, and said, 'What do you mean? He has sections of it, of course——' Suspicion began to seep through her mind. 'Did he walk out of here with my whole book?'

'Didn't you know about it?'

'Of course I didn't! Dad, did you let him steal my book?'

'Well, it was there on the table. And it's his book as well,' the professor pointed out. 'It was in a box, so I assumed that you had packed it up for him to take.'

'I put it away so I didn't have to explain it to anyone who got curious during tea! Dad, how could you let him do it?'

He said, with dignity, 'I assumed that you had discussed it with him, Mallory. You are working together, after all.'

Mallory climbed down off the stool and went into the living-room. For a moment, she tried to deny what she saw, but she had to admit that her father was quite correct. The table in the corner was bare, and the box that had held the book was gone.

# CHAPTER FIVE

MALLORY dialled Duncan's telephone number every fifteen minutes until midnight, and was greeted each time with the monotonous buzz that said the line was busy. 'Off the hook, more likely,' she grumbled, and finally gave up and went to bed. She'd catch him first thing tomorrow and demand an explanation. If that so-and-so thought he was being helpful by kidnapping her manuscript, she thought, he would soon find out just how much trouble one smart-aleck sociology expert could get himself into!

But in the morning, when she tried to telephone again, there was no answer, just an endless ringing in what must be an empty apartment. 'Seven-thirty in the morning,' she mumbled. 'I'd thought that Caroline would still be getting her beauty sleep!'

'That's not a fair thing to say,' her father said mildly. 'Anyone who works the evening-shift can't be called lazy if she sleeps late in the mornings.'

'I didn't say she was lazy. And in any case, she's not there, either. Or at least she isn't answering the telephone, and I let it ring a dozen times.' Mallory refilled her coffee-cup and sat down at the kitchen table.

'Here,' her father recommended. 'Read the newspaper and get your mind off it. There's no point in worrying, anyway. Duncan isn't going to do anything foolish with that book.'

'At least, nothing that *he* thinks is foolish,' Mallory grumbled, but she took the section of the newspaper. 'Has Matt come downstairs yet?'

'Haven't seen him.' The professor looked up at the clock. 'He went to bed early last night, too.'

A twinge of uneasiness gripped Mallory. 'I'd better go check on him.'

'He's probably singing in the shower, and is so charmed by the concert that he's forgotten what time it is.'

'Nevertheless——' She ran up the stairs, planning to give Matt a first-class lecture on responsibility if he had overslept.

He was coming down the hall towards the stairs, slowly, his hands in his bathrobe pockets. His eyes were red-rimmed, his shoulders were slumped, and he looked as if he hurt all over.

'I was just coming down to talk to you,' he said.

'What's the matter with you this morning?' Mallory asked. 'Did someone sock you in jaw? It looks swollen.'

Matt shook his head sombrely. 'I have a headache and a fever, and my throat hurts like blazes.'

It must be bad, she thought, if he didn't even respond to teasing. She reached up and laid a hand on his forehead. He was right; his skin was hot to the touch.

'Say "Ah",' she ordered.

He did, obediently, and after she had peered at his throat, he asked, 'What does it look like?'

'It isn't going to win any beauty contests. How long has this been going on, Matt?'

He sighed. 'A couple of days. My throat's been scratchy, but I thought if I got a good night's sleep, it might go away.'

'Well, obviously that didn't work. Go back to bed, and I'll bring you something to eat.'

He turned obediently towards his room. 'I'm not hungry.'

'Now I know you're sick. It's not like you to turn down food. Would you like some tea, at least?'

He tried to smile. 'Tea is your solution to everything, isn't it, Mallory?'

No, she thought. Yesterday's tea hadn't solved a thing!

When she brought up a tray a few minutes later, Matt was lying flat on his back atop the blankets, still wearing his robe. She sat down on the edge of his bed. 'You've been trying to do too much, Matt,' she said. 'With all these extra activities, it's no wonder you're sick.'

He didn't even argue. He sat up and sipped the cup of tea, and made a face.

'Dad's going to call the clinic as soon as it opens.'

He looked alarmed. 'I don't need a doctor, for pete's sake! Dad's got classes. He's too busy to hang around here waiting on me——'

'He doesn't have classes this morning. And you're obviously not in any shape to drive yourself over to the clinic. You'll notice I'm not planning to argue about whether you're going to see a doctor.' She stood up. 'I'll report you sick at school.'

'I've got a test in chemistry this afternoon,' he muttered.

'It will wait for you to get back.' She glanced at the clock on his bedside table. 'I'd better get going, or I'll be late myself.'

The professor called at lunch time to tell her that the doctor thought Matt probably had mononucleosis. 'No big deal,' he said cheerfully. 'He can't do anything strenuous for a while, but it shouldn't be any big problem.'

Mono, Mallory thought with a groan, was the bane of teenage kids. It was a simple virus, and it was seldom actually dangerous. But the only treatment was rest, and sometimes the exhaustion dragged on for months. If Matt was ill all summer...

The professor could afford to sound cheerful about it, she told herself. His summer lecture schedule was already planned; he would be gone for weeks at a time.

Melinda looked up sympathetically from the chopped lettuce on her tray. 'I suppose Matt was going to help serve tables at your party next week,' she said.

'It's two weeks—isn't it?'

'Nope. The junior-senior prom is this weekend. Mallory, not even you can be calm enough to forget that you have twenty-four people coming to dinner a week from Saturday night.'

Mallory wanted to put her head down on the table and cry. I'm so tired, she thought. I'm tired of being responsible. And if Matt is sick all summer...

She tried to convince herself that Matt had probably just picked up the flu. Or, even if it was mononucleosis, it might be a very mild case, as the nurse had said. It certainly didn't mean that he would be at home for months, or be an invalid needing constant care.

'Don't be an idiot,' she told herself firmly as she walked back to her classroom. 'You don't have to go looking for trouble—enough of it will find you, without you having to seek it out.'

She opened her classroom door, saw that her chair was occupied, blinked and looked again, and then groaned. 'Truer words were never spoken,' she muttered.

Duncan looked up from the test paper he had been reading. 'Were you talking to me?'

'Not exactly. I was speaking of trouble in general. Why did you steal my manuscript last night? I told you I wasn't done with that chapter, but if you had insisted, I'd have given it to you——'

'I know.' He didn't sound interested. 'I didn't want the chapter.'

'You wanted the whole book?' She put her hands on her hips. 'Well, let's get this straight right now, Duncan

Adams. You aren't doing me any favours by taking over this project. That is *my* book and I intend to be the one who writes it. I don't plan to let you steal it from me!'

'Who's stealing? Did you make that outfit?' His gaze wandered over her, inspecting her yellow and white plaid jacket and the matching skirt that draped gently. It wasn't new, but she had teamed it with a new silk blouse that made the entire outfit more stylish.

The assessing look was making her nervous. She wondered if she had spilled her lunch all over the front of the suit. 'Yes, I did. What's it to you?'

He smiled suddenly. 'Well, you certainly look like a ray of sunshine. Of course, you don't sound much like one. I came to observe your independent-living class. You did invite me to come, if you remember.'

'I never thought you'd actually do it.'

'Stop grumbling.'

'What about the book, Duncan?'

'We'll talk about the book later. You have students wanting your attention at the moment.'

'I can see that. This isn't the class you're interested in, anyway. This is sewing——'

'I thought it might be,' he said mildly, 'since most of them are waving needles in the air.'

'If you'd like to go have coffee in the teachers' lounge, and come back at two——'

'No, thanks,' he said comfortably. 'I had enough trouble finding my way here; I wouldn't want to venture out into that jungle again.'

Mallory sighed and gave up. It was pointless to argue with him, that was sure. If Duncan said he didn't want to leave, it would take a crane to move him. She went off to one of the kitchen units and started the coffee-pot. The suggestion that Duncan go to the teachers' lounge had made her long for a cup of coffee herself.

The rich smell of the brew drew him there within minutes. He pulled up a high stool to perch on and watched as she piled egg shells into a basket.

'I thought you were using whole eggs,' he said.

Mallory wrinkled her nose. 'Some of the places these eggs go, they wouldn't smell so good after six weeks.'

'So you patiently poke holes in the shells and blow the contents out? When do you find time?'

'My beginning foods class did that this morning. They loved doing it, but of course it looked like enough scrambled eggs to feed the entire freshman class.'

'You've got a lot of shells there.'

'Two dozen. I've been known to break a few myself before I get them all handed out.'

'I was wondering if there were that many kids in this class.'

'About twenty. Actually it only takes half as many eggs as there are kids, because each baby is assigned to two parents. It increases the challenge when they have to co-operate. Sometimes they nearly come to blows over deciding whether it's a girl or a boy.'

'I bet they have a lot of fun with it.'

'At first, of course. Last fall a few of them got the wild idea of announcing the births in the school newspaper. "Heather Bates and Max Ryan are the proud parents of a son, Eggbert." The only problem is, the article didn't make clear that the babies were only pretend, and when the newspaper hit the parents' mailboxes, the parents hit the roof.'

'And you've got the nerve to do it again?'

'The newspaper adviser has been warned to exert some censorship for a while.'

Duncan picked up a shell. 'What makes the eggs that funny colour?'

Mallory looked around, and then said softly, 'A careful soaking in strong tea. But don't tell the kids that—I only do it so I can make sure they have the same egg all the way through.'

'You'd be tough to fool.'

'Was that a compliment? Even if it wasn't, it's true. Two years of teaching at this level could make a saint cynical.'

He looked her over, quizzically. 'You mentioned before how unhappy you are here.'

'Not unhappy, really. But I have been thinking about making some changes in a few years.'

'Why wait? If you're positive you don't want to spend the rest of your life teaching high school home economics, why not do something about it now?'

'Can't.'

'Finances?'

'No. But Chandler College doesn't offer a master's programme in home economics.'

There was a brief silence. 'There are other schools, you know,' Duncan pointed out, as if he was talking to an infant. 'Are you too timid to leave this town? Or are you on probation for burglary, or something?'

She smiled. 'Of course not! And I'm not afraid to leave here. But until Matt is through high school, I'm responsible.'

Duncan's eyebrows escalated. 'Seems to me that Matt is a pretty level-headed kid. He can take care of himself.'

'Matt is my brother, not yours. I think it's up to me to decide what's right.' Why hadn't she just said something casual, she wondered, and pushed the subject aside? And why did Duncan think it was any of his business?

'And in the meantime, you're going to sit here and let yourself be wasted,' he murmured, looking around the big room.

It made her furious. She forced herself to take it lightly, and laughed. 'The last man who told me that followed it up by announcing that I should stop working and use my talents to make a comfortable home for a man who was out bettering the world.'

'And you objected to that?' There was a humorous quirk to his mouth. She was glad; he had obviously got the message that the subject of Matt was closed.

'I got the impression that he meant himself, and that he intended for me to put dinner on the table every night promptly at seven, wash his socks as soon as he took them off, and produce a baby once a year——'

Duncan swallowed a smile. 'And you didn't like the idea? I can't think why.'

Mallory went on ruthlessly, 'And never bother him with nonessential topics such as, *"I need more money for food if you insist on eating steak every night"*, *"I'd like to go to a party next weekend"*, or *"I want more than this out of life, you jerk!"'*

'Ah,' he said, on a note of discovery. 'I see what you're doing now. You're teaching seditious nonsense to these girls, filling their heads full of dreams, instead of instructing them about a woman's proper place in the world——'

'That was what he said. You almost got the tone of voice right, too.'

The bell rang, and girls rushed to shove their projects back into the bins and baskets. The room emptied in a matter of moments. Mallory carried her coffee-cup back to her desk, closing cupboard doors along the side of the room where the girls had been working.

'What happened to him?' Duncan set the basket of eggs on her desk blotter.

'My friend with the definite views? He married a little mouse. They have four kids now, and the last time I saw them he told me, "Meet my wife, the dumb blonde." Ordinarily I'd feel sorry for a woman in that position, but she seemed to think it was an endearment.'

'I'm very happy that you didn't marry him,' Duncan said.

'Are you? A lot of men don't see it quite the same way.'

'Oh, that wasn't what I meant at all,' he assured her airily. 'You would have ruined the poor guy's life. He'd probably have committed suicide by now. Or murder.' He was perfectly straight-faced, but the laughter in his eyes threatened to boil over at any minute.

Mallory decided not to dignify that with an answer. She sat down on the corner of her desk with her back to him.

The kids enrolled in Mallory's independent-living class trickled in and took their seats at the horseshoe-shaped table. One of them, a strapping football player wearing a jersey with his name and a number blazoned across the back, spotted the basket of eggs and grabbed one. 'Hey, look!' he announced to his friends, and began tossing the shell into the air. 'I'm playing with the baby!'

'For the next three minutes, that's a game,' Mallory told him mildly. 'As soon as the bell rings, it becomes child abuse.'

He looked astounded, but he put the egg back in the basket and sat down.

Duncan raised an eyebrow a trifle, but he made no comment.

'Who's that?' a red-headed girl asked Mallory. She was staring at Duncan.

'The gentleman has normal hearing,' Mallory told her. 'You might try asking him instead of me.'

The bell shrilled, and Mallory slid off the corner of her desk. 'Your preliminary budgets are due today,' she reminded.

There was a collective groan. 'Money's my worst thing,' one of the girls said.

'Really? You sure know how to spend it,' the boy sitting next to her retorted.

Mallory cut the exchange off. 'Hand in one copy, keep the other so we can discuss this project as a group.'

'I still want to know who he is,' the redhead repeated, staring at Duncan.

Mallory reconsidered the idea of letting Duncan speak for himself. It might not be wise, she thought. 'Dr Adams from the college is joining us today to observe how this class operates.'

'I thought you said he could talk,' the girl protested.

'I can,' Duncan assured her. 'But this is Miss Mitchell's classroom, so she gets to do the talking.'

'I'm glad there's something you're willing to let me do,' Mallory muttered.

He smiled at her. 'Miss Mitchell and I are working on a project together,' he added cheerfully. 'I am here to observe the egg-baby experiment, and you are all a very important part of the research that we're doing.'

'Does that mean we're like guinea pigs?' the girl asked.

'No. You're a study group.' Mallory picked up the top sheet off the stack of homework papers. 'John, give us the figures on your budget plan.'

The football player shuffled pages, shifted in his chair, cleared his throat. 'Well, I know a place where I can rent a furnished apartment——' he began.

Two minutes later a squabble had erupted. 'What about laundry?' the redhead asked. 'Clothes don't come clean accidentally, you know. It costs money for the launderette and the bleach and the detergent——'

'I put that in the food section.'

'With the food?' the girl said incredulously. 'Why?'

'Well, you buy the soap stuff in the supermarket with the food, so——'

'Then you'd better figure your food allowance again,' someone else chimed in. 'You don't have enough money here to feed a parakeet, much less a horse like you!'

'Let's not get personal,' Mallory intervened and turned the subject.

Duncan didn't say a word in the half-hour discussion of budgeting processes, but Mallory could see from the corner of her eye that the sceptical look he had displayed at the beginning had vanished within minutes. She put the pile of budgets in her briefcase and handed out another blank worksheet. 'Let's try it again, from scratch,' she said. 'Now that you've had the benefit of other people's reasoning and research, it should be easier this time.'

'That's what you say,' the football player muttered.

Mallory ignored him. 'Now for the real business of the day,' she said. 'We've been talking about the egg-babies for a week, so all we really need to do today is review the highlights. You've had a chance to make a few preparations, the same way parents do during a pregnancy, and now you're ready to take over the responsibility—right?'

The answers came in a chorus. They were mostly wisecracks. It was just as well, Mallory thought, that she couldn't hear each one individually. She could remember well enough the first time she had tried this experiment, and the fear of failure that she had felt on the day the egg-babies were handed out. She had nearly panicked because no one seemed to be taking the project seriously. It was weeks later, after the experiment was over, that she realised how the psychology of responsibility worked, and how long it took.

She walked around the room, placing an egg carefully on the table in front of each couple. Some of the girls reached out eagerly for the 'baby'; most of the boys grimaced or leaned back in their chairs, as far away as they could get.

'The rules are the same as they would be with an infant,' she reminded. 'Your baby cannot be left alone at any time—day or night, school day or weekend. If neither of you can be within hearing distance of the baby, then you must locate a reliable babysitter to take over the obligation. You will have to co-operate in making decisions and taking responsibility.' Duncan, she noticed, was inspecting the toe of his shoe, as if trying to ignore what he was hearing. He would soon see, she thought. She hadn't expected this idea to work the first time she'd seen it done, either. 'If any person in the school feels that your egg-baby has been mistreated or abused, your conduct can be called into question. If you——'

'Have you ever done this before?' the football player asked.

'Of course I have, John. You must remember how the kids taking this class last semester walked around school with their egg-babies in baskets and pouches—'

'No, I mean you personally, Miss Mitchell.' He stared doubtfully at the buff-coloured egg that lay in front of him, as if he was suddenly afraid of it. 'Have you ever had to carry one of these things around?'

'No, I haven't. But I have done a great deal of research on egg-baby experiments, wherever they've been done. You're in good hands, John. I know what I'm doing.' Duncan, she noticed, was trying to hide a smile. 'Are there any questions?'

The football player sat up suddenly and picked up the egg. His female partner squealed in protest and tried to grab it out of his hand. 'Fair is fair,' he announced. 'And I think if we have to carry these silly eggs around, you should do it too, Miss Mitchell. Show us what we're supposed to do, by example. That's the most effective way——'

'John, I do not have to sew every pattern a student uses in order to prove that I know what I'm talking about when it comes to dressmaking. I do not have to take part in every experi—'

'Have you ever had a baby?'

She flushed a little, in spite of herself. 'Of course not.'

'Then how can you teach us about it?'

Another voice chimed in. 'Yeah, the whole point is to teach us that we can't learn everything from books.'

Mallory would have liked to push the whole bunch of them out of the nearest window. This was the closest to a classroom mutiny that she had ever come in two years of teaching, and of course Duncan had to be there to see it!

'If it's such a wonderful experiment,' a third student began, 'and if you're using us as a research project, isn't it only fair that you do it yourself, too?'

The football player turned to Duncan. 'Can you give us one good reason why Miss Mitchell shouldn't be part of this experiment?' It was obviously a challenge.

Mallory held her breath. Get me out of this, she pleaded silently.

Duncan grinned. 'Not one,' he said cheerfully.

Mallory made a face at him.

'Wait a minute,' the redhead chimed in. 'He should have to do it, too. If they're in this together——'

Duncan squirmed just a little in his chair.

'Well?' Mallory asked maliciously, enjoying his discomfort. Good enough for him, she thought. He should have seen that one coming! That will teach him to take sides with a bunch of kids. 'What about it, Dr Adams? Are you ready for a little experimental parenting? I warn you, six weeks is a long time.'

For a moment their eyes locked, Duncan's brown and Mallory's blue, in a challenge to see who would back down first.

'I'm game,' he said. 'And you, Miss Mitchell?'

She could not refuse, she knew, or the respect she had worked so hard to earn from her students would be shattered. 'Absolutely.' She handed him an egg, then took a second one out of the basket and set it on her blotter.

'Not fair!' the redhead cried. 'If we have to co-operate so do you. One baby between the two of you.'

There was a chorus of approval. Mallory shuddered a little, inwardly, and put one shell back in the basket. 'Very well,' she said, and tried to tell herself that it was all in the day's work. It might even be good for her; she could probably write about it better if she had actually been a part of the experiment.

She tried not to look at Duncan, but out of the corner of her eye she could see that he was carefully cradling the eggshell—our eggshell, she reminded herself—in the palm of his hand, as if rocking it.

She rushed on, trying to regain control of her classroom. 'You have the handbooks that you were given last week, with space to keep records. Make sure that you do so. Tomorrow when you come to class you'll——' she corrected herself, almost unwillingly '—we will compare notes on the first day with the babies.'

'Is he going to be here every day?' the redhead asked, nodding her head towards Duncan.

'Why don't you ask him?' Mallory snapped, goaded beyond all patience.

Duncan stretched, balancing the egg-baby neatly. He looked over at Mallory, and she could see nothing but good humour in his eyes. 'Just as often as I can,' he said. 'I have a feeling this is going to be too good to miss.'

# CHAPTER SIX

MALLORY was still smouldering when the final bell rang and, for a full five minutes afterwards, she did her best to ignore Duncan. But Duncan, she found, was very hard to ignore.

'I think we should name her Alexandra,' he announced.

'The egg? Who says it's a female, anyway?'

Duncan's smile flashed. 'I do, and I have never had any trouble telling girls from boys.'

'I'll just bet you haven't,' Mallory muttered. 'You've probably had experience with thousands.'

'That's unfair. What sort of man do you think I am, anyway?'

'I don't think you want to hear my answer, Duncan. Why don't you take the damned egg and get out of here?'

Duncan looked hurt. 'I never thought you'd be the kind of mother who would abandon her own——'

'Duncan, get out. I'm going home.'

'I thought you wanted to talk about the book.'

Mallory opened her mouth, and then closed it. She'd almost forgotten about the book. 'As a matter of fact,' she said, 'yes, I do. What makes you think that it's all right with me for you to take it over? It's my book, and I have no intention of letting you push me aside and steal my ideas——'

Duncan leaned against the corner of her desk and folded his arms across his chest. It was a very nice broad chest under the tweedy jacket, Mallory noticed absently.

'I told you before,' he said. 'I'm not stealing anything. I merely removed the book from a chaotic working
environment to a quiet one in which we can accomplish
something. You needn't think I plan to do all the work;
I'm not a martyr.' He sounded mildly offended at the
idea. 'Now get your coat, because we've got a job to
finish.'

Mallory blinked. All right, smarty, she told herself.
Get yourself out of this one! Duncan had neatly hedged
all of her objections, and he was holding her manuscript
hostage. If she didn't go with him, he had the book and
could use it any way he pleased. If she did go with him...

'Where are we going?' she asked doubtfully.

'To my apartment, where it's quiet. To work,' he
added, without even looking at her.

Mallory's face burned. He needn't have made it so
painfully clear that he had no desire to do anything else
with her, she thought. As if she wanted to have a repetition of that night in the pizza house car park, when
he had kissed her!

It was the first time she realised how often she had
thought about that kiss in the last thirty-six hours.

Only because it was so unexpected, and so un-
welcome, she told herself firmly. And so embar-
rassing—being kissed that way in public, with an
audience looking on. That was the only reason it had
stayed in her mind so firmly, as if every detail was etched
into her consciousness. She could almost feel the supple
leather of his glove on the nape of her neck right now,
she thought, the heat of his hand burning through to
warm her skin. And the coolness of his mouth in the
cold April breeze...

Good grief, she thought, you sound as if you've never
been kissed before!

'Caroline's on duty tonight,' he went on. 'We'll have the place to ourselves. We can order in some food and really make progress with the book.'

'I can't, Duncan. Matt's sick, and I really need to go home——'

'I know all about Matt.'

She blinked. 'How?'

'The professor told me when I called to inform him that you wouldn't be home this evening.'

'Well, wasn't that thoughtful of you!' Mallory cooed.

Duncan didn't take the bait. 'Your father can manage chicken soup, Mallory. Or don't you think he can do anything at all unless you're there to hold his hand?'

She sighed. 'Is that a challenge? All right, I'll come with you.'

'Good. Let's go get to work on a book.' He held Mallory's coat for her, picked up her briefcase, and handed her the egg. 'You can carry the baby,' he announced.

'Male chauvinist.'

His eyebrows raised. 'Unless you'd rather carry your briefcase,' he pointed out. 'It weighs a ton. What do you have in here, anyway—your collection of wrought iron?'

'No. Just a lot of papers to grade.'

Duncan shook his head. 'You're going to have to learn to organise your time better, you know,' he announced as they walked through the halls. 'You'll have to cut back on the homework assignments, or something.'

'Why? So I have time for you?' It was nasty, and she knew it. Nevertheless, there was a little spot of warmth around her heart at the idea that Duncan thought she was working too hard, and was concerned.

He looked offended. 'Of course not. But you really should spend some time with the baby.'

'You got us into this; you can take care of the egg.' It was uncompromising. Idiot, she told herself. You asked for that.

'I wish you would stop referring to Alexandra as "the egg",' Duncan complained. 'It could leave emotional scars.'

'That will be nothing compared to the scars you have if you don't stop calling it Alexandra, as if it was a real person!'

'Isn't that the whole idea? Alexandra Adams,' Duncan mused. 'It has a rather nice ring, I think. You're right, of course, about me being a chauvinist, at least when it comes to naming children. I admit it. I firmly believe they should carry their father's name——'

Mallory paused beside her car. 'If you're quite finished with the lecture,' she said acidly, 'would you like to give me directions so Alexandra and I can get to your apartment?'

He rewarded her with a smile that was like the sun coming out from under a cloud. She still hadn't regained her balance by the time she parked her car in front of the new brick apartment building directly across from the main administration building of Chandler College.

She looked down at the delicate egg-shell, nestled in the seat. 'Alexandra, this man is dangerous,' she muttered, and caught herself. Her association with Duncan was becoming a threat to her mental health, she thought. After all, being seen talking to an egg would be enough to get her hauled away for psychiatric care. And it would all be Duncan's fault.

Of course, she thought, he probably wouldn't have the grace to admit that. He'd probably be too busy laughing as the men in the white coats took her away.

It was a very ordinary apartment, typical of the cheaply built housing that had sprung up around Chandler College in the last few years, in a vain attempt to accommodate a growing population of married students and young faculty members. There was an anonymous beige living-room, with a tiny kitchen tucked in one end and a brief hallway off to the side that could only lead to the bedrooms and bath. That was it. The only unusual feature was a tiny balcony off the living-room, and even it was identical to the balconies of the apartments above and below. It was small, compact, and neat, and it looked somehow as if no one lived there at all.

It tugged at Mallory's heart. It would be so easy, she thought, to make it into a home. A little colour here and there—a bright piece of art on the wall, some brilliant place mats on the kitchen table, some patterned fabric cushions scattered here and there. Some plants to give the place a little personality, and a few personal items...

It's none of my business, she told herself firmly. It's no wonder if they've done nothing to make the apartment special. To them, it's only a place to live for a while, not a home.

Did Duncan and Caroline have a home somewhere? she wondered. Was that part of the reason that Duncan was going back East for a summer's research? Did he intend to return to Chandler at all? Or, once that work was done, would he go on to some other town, some other college, some other project?

Some other woman, she caught herself wondering, and bit her lip. What had brought that insane idea to mind? As if there was anything more than a manuscript that lay between them!

One kiss, she thought. She was carrying on about that as if he'd tried to seduce her!

Duncan asked, 'Did you and Randy patch up your quarrel?'

She blinked, uneasily wondering if he had read her mind. 'We didn't quarrel,' she said, airily. 'I told you that Randy and I are just friends.'

'Ummm.'

'What does that mean?'

He grinned, dropped his jacket over the back of a chair, and pulled his tie loose. 'Anything you want it to. Want a cup of coffee?'

'Sure. It'll help me stay awake.'

'Caroline left some doughnuts, too. Remember the undergraduate days of caffeine pills and tons of empty carbohydrates and cramming for finals week?'

'I never did things like that,' Mallory said righteously. 'I always studied when I was supposed to, and I never had to worry about finals.'

He grinned. 'And I'll bet all your friends called you Saint Mallory when you pulled down the perfect grades.'

She unbent a little. 'Well, something like that. I've done more cramming in the last two weeks on this book than I ever did in college.'

The doughnuts were covered with powdered sugar, a thick, pasty coating. He set a plate of them on the coffee table, and handed her a big mug full of dark, steaming liquid.

'I love these things,' Mallory murmured, breaking a doughnut in half. 'They're so noxiously sweet and messy, and absolutely awful for the diet—that's what makes them wonderful.'

Duncan was watching her with an expression that she'd never seen before. His eyes were intense, and he looked as if the sight of her was slightly painful.

'What's the matter?' she asked. 'Do I have powdered sugar all over my face?' She licked her upper lip, nervously.

He closed his eyes, briefly, and then said, sounding just a little angry, 'Let's start by going over the chapters

I've rewritten. When those meet your approval, then we're done with them.' He handed her a stack of pages, and Mallory kicked off her shoes and curled up on the end of the couch with the manuscript on her lap.

She had glanced through each chapter individually, as he had brought them back to her, but this was the first time she had read the entire section and thoroughly studied his work.

Duncan paced the floor while she read. Was he that nervous about what she would think of his suggestion? she wondered. It surprised her.

There were very few changes she wanted to make, and when the last page was approved and handed back to him, she looked up with something in her eyes that was almost awe. 'You make it look so easy.'

Duncan shrugged. 'You did all the work. It was just a case of smoothing your logic out here and there, and sometimes of finding a better or clearer example.' He sat down beside her. 'Here's where the tough part begins,' he warned. He dropped another section of the manuscript in her lap and leaned over to point out a questionable paragraph.

Mallory sighed. 'I was afraid of this.' She reached for another doughnut. 'This is why you lured me up here to your lair, right?'

Duncan grinned, and then growled, playfully, 'That's right. I wanted to seduce you into making changes in these figures——'

She giggled, and a clump of powdered sugar fell off the doughnut and rolled down the front of her blouse. 'Darn it,' she muttered, brushing futilely at the trail of white dust on the silky fabric.

Duncan made a small choking sound, and she looked up at him, startled. 'What's the matter with you?' she asked.

'Oh, hell,' he muttered. 'Let's be honest, Mallory. The only figure I have the least interest in talking about is yours. And the only seduction I have in mind... Leave the powdered sugar, darling. I'll be delighted to remove it for you——'

He bent his head, and the first brush of his tongue against the silky fabric that covered her breast was like a spear to her heart. 'Duncan, for heaven's sake, stop being silly——'

His hand tightened at her waist, and long fingers caressed her ribcage. The light pressure seemed to squeeze all the breath from her. 'Silly, is it?' he murmured. The hand moved slowly, inexorably upward to cup her breast. It felt to Mallory as if there was nothing at all between the heat of his hand and her delicate skin. His touch seemed to burn away the silky blouse and the lace of her bra, and leave her naked to the knowing caress of those strong fingers.

His other arm lay lightly about her shoulders. His grip tightened, pulling her away from the couch cushions until she was balanced lightly against him, unable to find a hold of any kind to push herself away.

But did she want to escape him? Her head fell back against his shoulder, leaving her unaware that she had moved at all. She looked up into his eyes, and she sighed, a tiny animal whimper, the sound of surrender.

It was all the invitation he needed. He took her mouth gently at first, his tongue teasing against the softness of her lips until she relaxed and let him kiss her more deeply.

'You taste like powdered sugar,' he said, his voice rough. 'My sweet Mallory...'

She didn't want him to talk. She didn't want him to do anything that meant he would stop kissing her. She stroked his hair, touched with gold by the last rays of the afternoon sun, and murmured a protest when he released her lips and began to nibble at her throat, tiny love bites that led him down to the top button of her blouse.

'What——' she gasped, as the button slipped loose under his fingers.

'I just want to be sure you didn't drop any sugar here,' he whispered, and his tongue flicked at the hollow between her breasts. Mallory gulped in astonishment at the sensation of heat that radiated out from this intimate touch, searing her whole body, turning her into a torch that needed only a spark to start an all-consuming conflagration.

There was satisfaction in Duncan's tone as he said, 'You like that, hmmm?' He began to trace the outline of her bra with his tongue.

The doorknob rattled.

'Duncan!' Mallory gasped.

'It's probably the paper boy,' he murmured, and slid a finger under the lacy edge of the bra to caress the silken skin.

'Doesn't he just put the newspaper in the box downstairs?'

Duncan frowned. 'Now that you mention it——'

A key clicked in the lock, and Mallory sat up straight, clutching at the open neckline of her blouse. There was no time to fasten it; the best she could do was straighten the collar and hope that, if she sat very still, no one would notice that she was unbuttoned nearly to the navel.

When the door opened they were sitting close together on the couch, and Duncan was leaning over Mallory's shoulder, his finger pointing out a paragraph on the top page of the manuscript she held. To the casual observer, Mallory hoped, it would look as if they were absorbed in work. But her mind was spinning too much to even comprehend the subject of the chapter. Duncan's breath against her cheek was like a drug.

'Oh! I am sorry. I hope I'm not interrupting any-thing?' The voice was tremulous.

'Caroline?' Duncan sounded astonished.

So who else would it be? Mallory thought, with a sudden flare of irritated jealousy. Who else has keys to your apartment, Duncan, my dear? Just who were you expecting to come through that door?

Caroline was wearing grey slacks and a matching sweater, and a navy suede blazer. A bright-patterned scarf in red, grey and blue was twisted at her throat, and her blonde hair was loose around her shoulders. She looked gorgeous, and she obviously had not just come from hospital duty; the bags and boxes she carried made that apparent. She looked very happy, Mallory thought. Was that Randy's influence?

'The supervisor called earlier and said they wouldn't need me tonight, so I went shopping instead.' Caroline sounded as if she was apologising. 'I didn't think to call you, Duncan. I never imagined I'd be in the way——'

'Of course you're not,' Mallory said. 'We decided to work here because Matt's got sick, and it would be a problem to be at my house——' Stop babbling, she told herself.

'Is Matt your brother? I'm sorry to hear that he's sick. Nothing serious, I hope.'

Mallory shrugged. 'The doctor thinks it's mono.'

'Oh, that's a bit tricky. If you need any help with him, I'd be happy to pitch in, Mallory. I've seen a few cases in my time.'

'Caroline used to work in a hospital that specialised in adolescent medicine,' Duncan volunteered.

Mallory could hear the tension in his voice, but she hoped that Caroline would miss it, or assume that he was thinking about the book. 'Why did you get out of it?' she asked.

There was the barest pause, so slight that Mallory wasn't sure if she'd imagined it. Then Caroline said, 'A couple of years of that sort of thing is all the average person can take,' she said. 'Sick teenagers are the most trying patients of all, I believe. But I'd be happy to help out if you have trouble with Matt.'

'I doubt we'll have any problem,' Mallory said. 'Matt has always been healthy——'

'Those are the worst kind.' Caroline shifted her bags and boxes and picked up a doughnut.

'Caroline,' her brother said gently. 'We are trying to work, here——'

'Of course. I wouldn't want to interrupt that.' She smiled sweetly and crossed the living-room to the tiny hallway. She turned in the door, and said, in a dulcet tone, 'By the way, Duncan, you might want to go comb your hair. I can't think how you could have got powdered sugar all over it, but that is certainly what it looks like.'

She turned on her heel, and a moment later a door clicked shut.

'Damn!' Duncan said. His hand went experimentally to the back of his head, where Mallory's hands had rested caressingly only moments before.

Mallory pulled her left hand out from under the stack of manuscript pages and unfolded her fingers with difficulty. Her palm was coated with the sticky, doughy residue of the doughnut she had been holding when Duncan kissed her. She had forgotten all about it. 'Sorry,' she said miserably.

'Mallory, you're the only woman I know who can turn a doughnut into a deadly weapon. I bet when you peel an orange you're considered armed and dangerous!'

'Don't look at me like that. That little wrestling match wasn't my idea.'

'Oh, really?' Duncan's eyes were smouldering. 'Well, it might have been my inspiration, but I'm experienced enough to recognise full participation when I see it.' He ran a finger from the hollow at the base of her throat to her waist, parting the blouse. Mallory gasped and tried to pull it back together.

He laughed. 'Suddenly shy? You weren't doing that sort of thing a few minutes ago.'

'Caroline wasn't——'

'Caroline, hell! You're just scared, Mallory. You're scared to let yourself feel anything.'

Was he right? She had certainly been frightened, she thought; not so much of Duncan as of that unexplained heat that had flashed through her and made her desperate to find release. She stumbled to her feet and washed her hands at the kitchen sink, watching the remnants of the doughnut swirl down the waste disposal.

I don't think I'll ever eat another powdered-sugar doughnut in my life, she thought.

She buttoned her blouse with shaking fingers and sat down primly in a straight-backed chair. 'I plan to forget that this happened,' she said. 'Now, shall we get back to work?'

'We might as well,' Duncan said grumpily. 'Look, Mallory, I'm sorry about this little episode. In fact, I'm sort of glad Caroline came home, before we went any farther.'

Fury started to rinse in Mallory's throat. 'Oh?' she said. 'And just what else do you think would have happened?'

He snapped, 'We'd have been in my bedroom in a few minutes. You'd forgotten to be scared, you see, and I——' He sighed and rubbed the back of his neck as if it hurt. Then he said, more quietly, 'I'd like to think I would have had enough sense to quit. Dammit, I certainly ought to know better than to sleep with someone I'm working with!'

Mallory glared at him. 'And just who says I'd be interested in sleeping with you, anyway? Under any circumstances?' She gave a delicate little shiver. 'A kiss or two, yes. But anything more than that——'

He seized her shoulder and spun her around to face him. 'Don't be a hypocrite, my dear,' he said. 'You were with me every step of the way, until Caroline walked in. Did seeing her remind you of Randy?'

She was furious. 'Oh, how I wish I hadn't washed my hands,' Mallory mourned. 'I would like to smear that damned doughnut into your face!'

'Try it some day,' he threatened. 'And I'll hold you down and make you lick it off.' He paused, and then said, huskily, 'Damn, that sounds like fun. Here, Mallory, have a doughnut. Let's try it.'

The very idea of cleaning powdered sugar off his smoothly tanned skin with her tongue splashed embarrassed colour across Mallory's face. She turned away. 'I don't think we're likely to get much work done tonight, after all,' she said.

'Oh? With Caroline to chaperon, I think we would do much better than if we were left on our own.'

She didn't want to discuss that one. 'I'm going home now.' She stepped into her shoes, picked up her coat, and started for the door.

'Mallory——'

She raised her voice. 'Goodnight, Caroline!'

A cheerful answer came from the back of the apartment. 'Don't forget, if you have trouble keeping Matt under control, I'd be happy to help!'

'I'll remember. It's very kind of you to offer.' She fended Duncan off at the door. 'Don't walk me out,' she said. 'I'm more afraid of you than I am of the muggers.'

He grinned. It looked as if his good humour was restored, but Mallory wasn't quite convinced; there was a challenging sparkle in his eyes that left her feeling a little uneasy. 'Are you sure you don't want to take a doughnut along?' he asked smoothly. 'Just in case you need to defend yourself?'

He didn't call her; he didn't stop by the house; he didn't appear at school. She told herself it didn't matter, and went about her work with half her mind elsewhere, knowing that she was lying to herself.

Two days later, when she went into Matt's bedroom to tell him goodbye before she left for school, she found him lying pale and sweaty under the quilt, with only his nose and a pair of fever-bright eyes showing.

'Matt!' she exclaimed. 'What's wrong? You look awful this morning. Are you feeling sicker again, dear?'

He wouldn't look at her. 'No,' he muttered.

'Well, you certainly look rotten. I'm going to take your temperature——'

'Mallory, just leave it, OK?' he snapped. 'I'm all right.'

She ignored the protest. 'Sit up and let me look at you.'

He refused to move. 'Mallory——'

'Do you want me to call Dad up here?'

'No.' It was grudging. Slowly, Matt sat up, clutching the quilt to his chin.

Mallory turned from the bureau with the thermometer in her hand, and looked down at him with a puzzled frown. Something was not quite right here...

She took hold of a corner of the quilt and tugged.

Matt hung on to it with what looked like desperation. 'Spare a guy his modesty, would you, Mallory?' he howled.

'I want to look at the glands in your throat to see how swollen they are, Matt, that's all. You needn't worry that

I'll go any further. If I got turned on by adolescent male bodies, I'd be teaching physical education!' The remark served to remind her of a male body that was neither adolescent nor reluctant, a body that she hadn't seen for a couple of days, and that she was forced to admit that she missed. Mallory could have sworn as she felt a blush rise across her cheeks at the very thought of Duncan, and how it had felt to be held in those strong arms...

You sound like some kind of sex maniac, she told herself roughly. You haven't seen the guy for two days, and you're letting your imagination get out of hand. He couldn't possibly be as strong as you remember! Not that it had taken much strength to hold her, she admitted. She had, after all, not exactly been fighting to get free.

'All right,' Matt muttered. 'If you can look at my throat, then will you leave me alone?' He sounded pathetic.

'Poor guy,' she said. 'You're miserable at the idea of having to stay home, aren't you?' She put a gentle hand on his shoulder, and realised that what she felt through the quilt binding was neither bare skin nor a pyjama jacket. She glared down at him and tugged the quilt away.

'Matthew Mitchell, what in the hell are you trying to do?' she said, in a voice that should have been deadly.

Matt hung his head.

Mallory peeled the quilt back to reveal Matt's long body clad in a striped sweater and jeans. He hadn't got his shoes on yet, but he was wearing socks. When she thought about it, she remembered hearing a tiny scuffling sound when she had knocked on his door. He must have been scrambling back under the quilt so he wouldn't be discovered, she thought.

She sat down at the foot of the bed. 'All right, Matt. Spill it. You're not supposed to be up and dressed, and you know it.'

Matt sighed. 'I don't feel so awfully sick today, Mallory. And I thought if I did a little bit—like maybe went to school this morning—that I wouldn't get so far behind.'

'And you really thought that I wouldn't find out if you showed up at school? Matt, you're a nincompoop!'

'Of course I knew you'd find out. But I thought once I was there, and I was doing all right, that you wouldn't make me come home.'

'Look, it's not my idea to keep you out of school all week. The doctor told you to stay in bed.'

'I know, but——'

'But what?'

'Well, it isn't the doctor who's going to miss the debate team's trip tomorrow,' Matt burst out. 'He just laughed when I asked if I could go!'

'And you really thought that if you managed to make it back to school that I'd give you permission to go on the trip?'

He looked ashamed of himself. 'I thought it was worth a shot.'

'Oh, Matt! I know you were looking forward to going on the trip, but——'

'And I'm not giving up, either!' he announced fiercely.

'Well, you take your clothes off and plop yourself back in that bed and start scheming,' Mallory recommended. 'Maybe your next plan will work better.'

Matt made a face at her, but he sat up and pulled the sweater over his head. 'I guess I'm not feeling as well as I thought,' he mumbled. 'It wore me out just to get dressed.'

'Remember that, or I'll tattoo it on your nose,' Mallory threatened.

The professor was loading the breakfast dishes into the dishwasher. 'How's the animal this morning?' he asked.

Mallory groaned. 'Like an old lion who needs a keeper to prevent him from trying to make a kill,' she said. 'Does that make any sense?'

'Not much. Does it mean I have to cancel my classes again?'

'Fortunately, I think I know a good keeper.' I don't want to do this, she thought as she dialled the telephone. Well, perhaps it will be Caroline who answers.

It wasn't. Duncan's voice warmed instantly, as soon as she said hello. 'Mallory, my dear,' he said, 'I've been meaning to call and ask when you were going to let me visit the baby.'

Mallory glanced at the counter, where the tea-coloured egg-shell reposed in a small basket atop her stack of books. 'I don't remember making any agreement about visiting rights.'

'I think if we're going to be separated parents, we should at least go about it in a civilised manner,' he said.

'Well, I don't. And I called to talk to Caroline, anyway, not you.'

'Very well.' He sounded cheerful, and he put the phone down promptly. It made her wonder for a moment; it wasn't like Duncan to give in so easily. But then, it had only been a joke.

Caroline sounded slightly sleepy when she came to the phone. 'I hate to bother you,' Mallory said, 'but I caught Matt getting ready to sneak out of the house this morning. I'm afraid he needs someone to keep him in line——'

'Sounds familiar. I'll be over as soon as I'm dressed.'

'Oh, that wasn't what I meant at all! I just thought if I told him you'd be looking in on him some time today, he'd be too scared of getting caught to pull any more stunts.'

Caroline laughed. 'I haven't anything planned. Why don't I show him today what a tyrant I am? By tomorrow he'll promise you anything if only you won't make him have me around.'

Caroline, a tyrant? Gentle little Caroline, who never raised her voice? Mallory thought she'd believe that about the same time as the moon turned purple. But the fact remained that with someone—no matter who—in the house, Matt would be more likely to behave himself.

'It's putting you to an awful lot of trouble,' she began. 'But you have no idea how much I'd appreciate it.'

'My pleasure. Don't worry about a thing.' Caroline sounded brisk, efficient. Perhaps, Mallory thought, she was getting over that dreadful shyness. 'Duncan wants to talk to you again.'

Before Mallory could protest, he was back. His voice seemed to tickle her ear, almost as if he was whispering into it. 'About my seeing Alexandra,' he began. 'I want alternate weekends, holidays, six weeks in the summer—you'll have to bring her out East, but I'll return her at the end of August—and——'

'Don't be ridiculous, Duncan. This is an egg we're talking about.'

'Shush! You'll destroy her self-esteem. Do you mean to say that you don't want to let me see my daughter at all?'

'You've got it.'

'Well, so much for civil conversation,' he said cheerfully. 'Would you like to have dinner with me tonight, and we'll discuss it further?'

'No.'

'Why not?'

Mallory wanted to throw the telephone through the nearest window. 'Because I make it a rule never to get involved with men who have children,' she snapped.

'Not even when she's your child, too?' He didn't wait for an answer. 'I'll see you in class this afternoon.'

'What for?'

'So I can tell the students all about how, on the very afternoon Alexandra was born——'

'Hatched,' Mallory said drily.

'You left her in the front seat of your car for two hours, while you were in my apartment making brazen overtures——'

'I have never made a brazen overture in my life!' Mallory howled.

'I stand corrected. You don't know how. While you and I were necking——'

'You wouldn't tell them that.'

'I certainly would. I think they'd be interested in the sociological implications. See you this afternoon, Mallory.'

She would have thrown the telephone, then, except that she would have had to explain the broken window to her father. So she waited till she was on her way to school, and screamed instead.

## CHAPTER SEVEN

WHEN Mallory got to the cafeteria at lunch time, Randy Craig was already there, eating a square of dark gingerbread and talking to Melinda Anderson. He glanced up as Mallory approached, as if he had scented trouble.

He looks uncomfortable, she thought. It confirmed her suspicion that Randy had been going out of his way to avoid her all week. It irritated her, just a little. Was he afraid that she might make a scene? No chance, she thought. She'd scarcely had a moment to think about Randy all week. So much for the brilliant notion she'd had that night—the suspicion that she'd fallen in love with him! If she had, she'd know it by now. She would have missed him so badly this week that she would have ached for a sight of him.

Not that she wasn't happy to see him. She still had to talk to him about her independent-living class, and she wasn't about to let this opportunity pass. He might not give her another.

Not exactly the reaction of a woman in love, she told herself. That flash of jealousy she'd felt that night at the theatre must have been simply a fluke.

She set her tray down across from him. 'Haven't seen you around for a while, Mallory,' he said self-consciously.

Only because you've consistently been going in the other direction whenever you caught a glimpse of me, she thought.

'I need to talk to you,' she said.

His eyes shifted to the gingerbread crumbs on his paper plate. 'I'm afraid I'm pretty well tied up this afternoon——'

'It won't take long. In fact, we can discuss it here.'

Melinda stood up. 'I can take a hint,' she announced. 'Will five minutes give you enough time, or shall I take a walk around the block, instead of just to the kitchen?'

She didn't wait for an answer. Mallory spread ketchup evenly across her hamburger patty and said, 'About my independent-living class, Randy——'

For a bare instant, he looked startled, but before she could assess the expression in his eyes, it had vanished. Had it been surprise? Antagonism? A slight touch of fear? She wasn't certain.

'I don't want to give it up,' she went on earnestly. 'I know I'm overloaded as it is, and I appreciate your wanting to reduce my class load, but——'

'Independent-living? That's what you want to talk about?'

Mallory nodded. 'Please don't take it away from me, Randy. I started that class, and I don't want to hand it over to the social studies people.'

'You can't handle six classes a day, Mallory.'

'I know, but I could combine my sewing and textiles classes. The enrolments are low, and I can put them together——'

'You'll still be teaching them both. I know you.' He shook his head. 'The schedule's already drawn up for next fall, Mallory. I'm sorry.'

'Then change it! We both know that in a school this size schedules have to be flexible. That's the only thing I want next year, Randy.' Her blue eyes were huge and fixed on his face.

Randy sighed. 'All right. I'll try,' he said, and Mallory beamed with delight. 'I can't imagine why you want to keep that bunch,' he grumbled. 'They take six times as much patience and preparation as any other class——'

'That's exactly why,' Mallory pointed out. 'They're a challenge.' Besides, she thought, what hope would there be of selling her book if her school had decided she wasn't qualified to teach the class? And if it didn't sell, Duncan would be disappointed, an honest little voice in the back of her head reminded.

'And that's really what you wanted to talk to me about?' Randy asked. He sounded curious.

'What else did you think I had on my mind?'

He ducked his head. His face was flushed a bit. 'Caroline Adams,' he said sheepishly.

'Caroline?' She set her hamburger down and said carefully, 'We've never made any promises to each other, Randy, so I haven't any right to talk to you about Caroline.'

'Maybe not,' he muttered. 'But I was sure I was going to get dressed down for being a fool——'

'It was none of my business,' Mallory said crisply. 'It certainly isn't up to me to tell you you're being a blockhead, even if you are.' She smiled sweetly.

'Thanks. What you're really telling me is that Caroline Adams could have her pick of men, and it's foolish to think she might think I'm special.'

'I don't know,' Mallory said thoughtfully. 'She might not see a blockhead.'

Randy groaned. 'I made a donkey of myself. Don't tell me, I've already heard it every day this week.'

'From whom?' Mallory was honestly astounded.

'Who do you think? Melinda says that any man who can't see through a pair of gorgeous big green eyes——'

'Caroline's are brown, actually,' Mallory murmured.

'—is a dimwit,' Melinda said. She sat down and popped the paper cap off a tiny container of ice-cream.

'Now I ask you, Mallory, have you ever seen a woman as gorgeous as Caroline Adams who was anything but a flirt?' She dug into her ice-cream with the plastic spoon, as if wishing it was Caroline's face.

Mallory glanced at the big clock. 'Almost time for the bell,' she said. 'I think I'll avoid the crush in the halls.'

Randy jumped up. 'I'll come with you.'

Mallory raised an eyebrow. That's a switch, she thought. He's been dodging me all week, and now he wants to walk me to my room!

Oh, come on, she told herself. Maybe she had been just a little paranoid. Maybe he hadn't really been trying to avoid her. Randy was busy, she was busy, perhaps it was purely coincidental that days had gone by and they hadn't happened to run into each other.

'Are you all here?' he asked impatiently.

'Why? Did you say something?'

'I asked if you were still planning to help chaperon the prom on Saturday night.'

Mallory groaned. 'Do I have a choice?'

'Not really. We need every warm body. I suppose you've invited what's-his-name to come with you.'

'Do you mean Duncan? Well, I thought—Randy, hadn't we sort of planned to——' She was stammering like an idiotic schoolgirl. I'm being stood up! she told herself in disbelief. And he doesn't even realise he's doing it. He's forgotten all about our standing date to go to the dances together.

Randy didn't seem to hear. 'I thought I'd call Caroline and ask her to come with me.' His tone was defiant. Then he looked down at Mallory, and the certainty vanished from his voice. 'If I wouldn't be a fool to ask, that is,' he said. 'It's only a few days' notice. You don't think she'd be insulted?'

Mallory considered it. She could say that yes, she thought Caroline would be bitterly indignant, even humiliated, at the idea of being asked so late. It would be so easy, and then everything would go as Mallory had planned it—what seemed months ago.

But he had sounded like one of the kids, uncertain, hesitant. Mallory thought, it's not my idea of fun to go to a dance with a man who will be spending every instant thinking about another woman! And if you don't want him, she told herself, then you should let him go with grace.

'I don't think Caroline would be offended by the invitation, even if it is last-minute,' she said.

He looked as if she had just handed him an award. 'You think she'd like to go? Really?'

Mallory felt obliged to issue a warning. 'That's not quite what I said. Besides, she might be scheduled to work that night, and it's awfully late to ask someone to swap hours with her.'

He dismissed that with a snap of his fingers. 'Thanks, Mallory. I'll call her right away.'

Mallory struggled briefly with her conscience, and sighed. 'She's probably at my house,' she said.

He looked a little surprised, but he didn't question the information.

Caroline will probably jump at the chance, Mallory thought. She's no dummy, and she obviously knows what he thinks of her. And Melinda and I, Mallory told herself, will go to the prom together, and play at being wallflowers, and keep a sharp eye on the kids who want to sneak off into the dark corners—because if Randy is there with Caroline, he isn't even going to notice whether there is anyone else in the room!

She sighed. It was Wednesday, and Mallory Mitchell didn't have a date for Saturday night's dance. It would be the first time that had happened since she'd been a teenager herself.

She could always take Randy's suggestion, she reminded herself, and invite Duncan. The very idea of asking Duncan to a high-school prom sent her into whoops of laughter.

The independent-living class began without a glimpse of Duncan, and Mallory heaved a sigh of relief. His threat to come and tell the kids about her carelessness had been a bluff, she thought, just his way of getting a reaction from her. Typical of Duncan.

She refused to allow herself to admit to a prickle of disappointment. It was irritation, she decided. He still had possession of the book, and nothing was getting done on it. Sooner or later, she would have to track him down and demand the manuscript. She had almost hoped that he would show up today.

She passed out a page of homework questions for each student to answer. 'This is hard stuff, Miss Mitchell,' the football player informed her.

'I know, John. That's the reason I'm asking you to answer them. You have two weeks, and I recommend that you start tonight.'

'But I don't know stuff like what my parents think of mixed marriages!'

'Then perhaps you should ask them.' She perched on the corner of her desk. 'There are twelve questions here. You may select the ten you wish to answer. Each question calls for a well-thought-out, short essay.'

There was a collective groan. Mallory cut it off ruthlessly. 'There are no wrong answers, as long as you honestly believe what you say. Your logic and the evidence you use to back up your opinion are very important. Any questions?'

'Yes,' said a clear baritone from the back of the room. 'Can I borrow the list of questions to use in my classes?'

For the briefest instant, Mallory felt gladness flicker along her veins like lightning, tightening her throat and sending her heart on a wild race. It made her wonder for an instant how she could feel such overwhelming happiness at the mere sound of his voice. I'm glad I can ask him about the book, she decided finally. That's all it is. 'Good afternoon, Dr Adams,' she said, keeping her voice carefully polite.

Duncan rewarded her with a smile. 'Sorry I'm late,' he grinned. She tried not to look at him as he came across the room and leaned against the other corner of her desk. But she found that she had trouble ignoring him; all the energy in the room seemed to be concentrated on him. Today he was wearing grey trousers and a navy blazer; his white shirt was crisply pressed, and his striped tie was neatly knotted. 'I was delayed because I had to call for dinner reservations for this evening,' he said softly.

'Oh?' Mallory muttered under her breath. 'Did you find someone who was interested in going with you?'

Duncan looked down at her. For a moment she thought he intended to kiss her, heedless of their audience. Instead, he shifted his position and braced his hand against the desk blotter. It was resting uncomfortably near where Mallory was sitting; she could feel the warmth of his arm against her spine. She slid off the corner of the desk and began walking around the room. He smothered a smile and sat still, watching her.

She was never quite sure what she said in her lecture that afternoon. She knew that it held everyone's attention, and she was positive that one particular pair of coffee-coloured eyes never left her. He wasn't always looking at her face, she discovered once, to her embarrassment, when she turned suddenly towards him; at that moment he seemed to be appraising the way her ivory knit dress clung to her curves. She swallowed hard and turned her attention back to her class.

With only five minutes left, she knew she couldn't avoid the subject any longer. But surely, she thought, with such a limited time, he wouldn't start anything. She returned to her desk and said, 'Any problems with the egg-babies?'

Beside her, Duncan shifted and said, easily, 'Yes, as a matter of fact.'

'Duncan, please——' The words were out before she could stop herself. It was a panicky plea.

He smiled. 'But I don't want to take time away from the students. Perhaps we could discuss it later?' Under his breath, he added, 'I reserved a table for two. It's up to you, Mallory.'

Submit to blackmail? Oh, let him tell them, she thought furiously. What difference could it make whether that damned egg had been in the front seat of her car or on Duncan's coffee-table that afternoon? A lot of difference, she reminded herself. How could she expect the kids to take the experiment seriously when she hadn't?

But she had been serious about it, since that one lapse. The blasted egg had come to school with her every day. It spent the nights on her dressing-table, and even reposed on the kitchen counter while she cooked. The professor eyed it warily, as if wondering whether his daughter had gone crazy. Matt seemed to think it was cute that his sister was carrying an egg everywhere she went. Mallory herself was beginning to get darned tired of the exercise.

But it wasn't just a game, she reminded herself. It was a learning experience for this group of kids, and she couldn't allow it to be ruined for them. So Duncan wanted to take her to dinner—what difference did it make? As long as he was buying, she'd go along with it. He'd find that this brand of blackmail would end up hurting only his wallet.

'As you wish, Dr Adams,' she said calmly.

She saw triumph flare in his eyes, those liquid, animal-brown eyes, and her mouth went dry with a strange combination of anticipation and fear. Come on, she told herself. What could he do to her over dinner, in a public place?

He didn't move after the dismissal bell rang.

'Ready?' he said.

She nodded.

'You needn't look as if you've been condemned to the guillotine,' he said gently. 'I'm only going to follow you home, talk to your father a while, fit in a little work on the book, take you out to dinner——'

'I know.' She picked up her handbag and her coat.

'Then why are you looking at me as if you expect me to ravish you right here on your classroom floor?'

*Because I want you to!* The thought was so sudden, so unexpected, that Mallory turned brilliant red with fear that he might have read her mind. You idiot, she told herself. You're becoming just a little unbalanced!

'Sorry,' said Duncan. 'I didn't mean to embarrass you.' He rubbed a hand across his jaw. He looked ill at ease, more nervous than she had ever seen him before. 'What happened the other day was a mistake, Mallory——'

Because he made it a rule not to sleep with women he worked with, she wondered bitterly, or because he hadn't enjoyed kissing her at all? Either way, she thought, it wasn't very flattering.

'Why?' she asked, bluntly. 'Because you didn't get me into bed?' She let the silence draw out for a few moments, and then added, softly, 'You don't need to worry, Duncan. You're not my type, so you're in no danger from me at all.'

He was very still for a moment. Then he said, with an odd catch in his voice, 'I'm glad to know that, Mallory.'

She handed him her coat, and he helped her put it on. She was glad that she had her back to him, so that she didn't have to look at him. She didn't want him to see the suspicious wetness that she was fighting to blink out of her eyes.

Tears? she asked herself, fiercely. Why should she want to cry, just because Duncan Adams had told her he didn't intend to mess up their work on the book by becoming involved with her? Wasn't that what she wanted, too—to get the book done and see the last of him?

Matt was occupying the living-room, sprawled across the sofa with a pile of magazines beside him. He looked up with a weak grin when they came in.

'Hey, Caroline's not bad,' he told Mallory. 'She makes dynamite egg nog, and look at all the magazines she brought me! Just the kind of thing I like to read.'

So much for Caroline's reputation as a tyrant, Mallory thought. She smoothed his hair. 'Do me a favour, Matt.'

He eyed the box under Duncan's arm. 'Clear out, so you can work? Do I have to?'

'Yes, Matt.'

He got up and gathered his magazines together. 'Caroline didn't try to get rid of me,' he grumbled.

'Was she here all day?' Mallory asked.

Matt nodded. 'Till she had to go to work. She said she'd enjoyed herself. I didn't wear her out. We just played games, and talked, and listened to records.'

Caroline had incredible patience, Mallory thought. 'I'll put some coffee on,' she told Duncan.

There was a note from Caroline for her on the kitchen table, volunteering to stay with Matt again the next day.

'Caroline is a masochist,' Mallory muttered.

'What was that?' The professor had come in quietly. 'Something about Caroline? I thought she was a saint today, actually. She has quite a way with kids.'

Mallory looked at him in surprise. 'How do you know?'

He raised an eyebrow. 'I came home at lunch time to check on Matt. Any objection?'

'Of course not. I just——' She was feeling incredibly silly. What did she think had happened, anyway—that her father was scheming to be alone with Caroline? With a sixteen-year-old chaperon, to boot! 'Duncan invited me out to dinner, Dad. But I thought I should make sure you and Matt have a good meal——'

The professor smiled. 'Have a good time, dear. Matt and I can manage perfectly well with frozen dinners.

That's what I was afraid you would say, Mallory thought. She filled two mugs with coffee and went back to the living-room.

Duncan had spread the manuscript out on the table. Matt was hovering in the doorway, watching him work. 'I didn't know you'd been to Vienna, Duncan,' he said. 'Caroline told me——'

'Matthew.' She put a gentle hand on his shoulder.

He scowled. 'I'm leaving.'

Mallory ignored him and pulled a section of the manuscript across the table towards her. She sipped her coffee and started to work, longing for the peace and quiet of the afternoon they'd spent at Duncan's apartment. Before everything had fallen apart, they'd got a lot of work done.

Mallory thought sombrely that if Duncan preferred to come back into the madhouse on Armitage Road rather than take another chance in his apartment, what had happened between them that afternoon must have really frightened him.

The very idea made her angry. One lousy kiss, she thought, and he's panic-stricken! He must be afraid that I'm the kind of girl who expects that he'll propose to me just because he kissed me once!

A proposal. Her heart thudded a little at the very thought. That husky voice of his—what would it sound like to hear him say, 'Mallory, will you marry me?'

Her pencil point dug convulsively into the page, so hard that it snapped off and went flying across the room.

Duncan looked up, and said mildly, 'I realise the manuscript is already getting a bit dog-eared. But if we could keep from making it worse——'

She ducked her head in embarrassment and snapped, 'It's hauling it around that does all the damage. If you had left the darned thing here where it belonged, it wouldn't be dog-eared.'

'Actually,' he said thoughtfully, 'I think what we really need is an office. If we had a place to spread this thing out and leave it, it would go together much more smoothly.'

She stared at him. 'An office? Now's a fine time to think of that. We've done most of the work, thank God.'

'Not by a long shot. But the end of this project can't come soon enough for me,' Duncan said repressively.

'Then why bother with dinner out? Let's just have a sandwich and keep working.'

'Because my mother taught me that a reservation is a sacred thing.'

'Then why don't you call her up and take her to dinner?'

He put his pencil down and looked at her thoughtfully. 'You're angry.'

'Congratulations!'

'Why are you so afraid to have dinner with me, Mallory? You'll be perfectly safe.'

That's what makes me angry, she thought, and was horrified at her own reaction. Surely she didn't want a repetition of the afternoon at his apartment! And yet . . .

'Of course,' Duncan mused, 'I could come back to class tomorrow and tell the kids about Alexandra. I think, on the whole, that it would be less trouble for us to have dinner.'

Mallory groaned. She had forgotten all about the egg. She pushed the manuscript away and went to the door of the television-room.

'Matt,' she asked sweetly, 'will you do me a favour?'

'Another one?'

'Yes, please.'

He looked at her warily. 'What is it?'

'Would you take care of the egg for me tonight?'

Matt grinned. 'You're afraid it's going to interfere with your work? Just what are you and Duncan up to in there?'

'It's nothing like that.' She kept her temper with an effort. 'I'm going out, and I don't want to take it along.'

'Alexandra,' Duncan said in a tone of long-suffering patience, 'is not an *it*.'

Mallory ignored him. 'Please, Matt?'

'Does this mean I have to eat Dad's cooking while you and Clyde go out to eat?'

She glared at him and hoped Duncan hadn't heard.

'Sorry about the slip,' Matt muttered.

'Clyde?' Duncan repeated.

'It's Matt's little joke,' Mallory said, giving Matt a repressive glare. 'Since you're so secretive about your first name, he decided the "C" must stand for Clyde.'

'Mallory——' Matt protested.

She cut in neatly, 'Now, about this favour, Matt.'

'I'm sorry, sister dear, but I can't babysit.'

'Why not?'

'Because you don't want the baby to get mono, and I'm still infectious till at least Friday. The doctor said.' He smirked at her, shifted his blanket, and turned his back.

'An egg can't catch mono!' Mallory yelled above the blare of the television set.

Duncan sighed and shook his head. 'Somehow I get the impression that you aren't taking this experiment seriously,' he said. He reached into the basket and picked up the egg-shell. 'I'm a little worried about Alexandra. She doesn't look as if she's getting enough sleep.'

I could tell him to take the egg and get out, Mallory thought. I could dare him to tell the kids what happened, he's a teacher himself, and he won't mess up another teacher's plans just for the heck of it. I could tell him——

But the fact was, she wanted to go to dinner with him. She wanted to spend the evening with him, just the two of them, without the noise and confusion of the house on Armitage Road. Surely, she thought, she could have one evening to remember? One evening in which the main topic of discussion wasn't tables and graphs and statistics, but Duncan and Mallory...

He picked up a felt-tipped pen, and a moment later he put the egg back in the basket with an air of satisfaction. 'She looks much more comfortable now,' he announced.

Mallory peered into the basket. He had drawn features on the egg-shell: closed eyes with heavy eyelashes, a small Cupid's bow mouth, and a curl of dark hair on top of the head.

'Now she looks just like her mommy,' he murmured. He sounded pleased with himself.

Mallory looked down at the egg. There were vague resemblances, she supposed—the dark curls, the thick eyelashes. It was a silly thing to bring this feeling of warmth to her heart! Duncan was no artist, that was for sure.

She heard him say something under his breath that sounded like, 'Very kissable,' but she wasn't sure that she hadn't imagined it. She stole a look at him, but he was concentrating on the manuscript.

They settled back into silence then. Mallory couldn't tell if Duncan was accomplishing much; she knew she wasn't. She kept hearing herself say, 'We've done most of the work, thank God.' Even though Duncan had disagreed, she knew that eventually the project must come to an end. And she knew that thankfulness would be only a small part of the feeling when the book was done. Mixed with it would be a bit of fear at the idea of the book going out of her hands, out into public. And some sadness, as well—sadness for the completion of a goal that was very important to her, and sadness that, just as the book would be gone from her everyday routine, so, too, would Duncan.

I'm actually going to miss this egotistical so-and-so, she thought, with a twinge of astonishment. He's crept into my heart...

Oh, don't be an imbecile, she told herself. You can't fall in love with a man on a few weeks' acquaintance. And certainly not Duncan. Not when you've spent nearly every minute together fighting!

But, she reflected, we weren't always fighting...

She stopped herself there, afraid to dwell on the moments when she had been in his arms. It was with a new thoughtfulness that she turned back to her work.

Duncan had reserved a table in the dining-room of a downtown hotel, the most elegant place the city had to offer. 'No pizza tonight?' she murmured as the hostess showed them to an oval table in a corner, dimly lit by a shaded candle. She was determined to keep the conversation light; the atmosphere in the dining-room was thick enough to cut, and Mallory had no intention of forgetting why she was there.

'I'm sure they can whip one up for you.' He didn't sound as if it would disturb him.

The hostess eased the table away from the semi-circular velvet-covered couch. Mallory looked at it doubtfully and decided she would only make a fool of herself by requesting a regular table instead.

Duncan seated himself beside her and adjusted the table in front of them. 'Are you comfortable?' he asked. 'Do you have enough room?' His arm brushed against her breast and lingered as he pushed the table away the fraction of an inch.

The gesture puzzled Mallory a bit. Surely he hadn't meant to do that, she thought. Not that the flirting gesture surprised her; Duncan, she was certain, knew all the moves. But that he would use them on her...

Unless it was purely habit, she thought, the kind of thing he did whenever he took a woman out, so that he scarcely remembered himself why he did it. Or, was she, perhaps, imagining it? It had only been a momentary touch, after all. And he had been pushing at the table——

Oh, stop it! she told herself fiercely. If you're going to analyse every move he makes all evening, you're going to drive yourself crazy.

'What do you recommend?' he asked, opening the menu.

See? she told herself firmly. He hadn't even noticed! 'They do wonderful shrimp Antoine here. But perhaps you don't like seafood?'

'I loved your scallops,' he pointed out.

'I didn't know if you really liked them, or if your mother taught you to be polite and clean your plate no matter what.'

He didn't answer, and eventually she looked up to see if he had even heard her. The menu lay forgotten in front of him; he was inspecting her, instead. The candle flames reflecting in his eyes looked like dancing devils, she thought.

'You're very pretty tonight,' he said. 'I like the way that neckline drapes and frames your face.' As if to prove his point, he flicked the hollow at the base of her throat with a careless finger.

Mallory gulped. The finger casually slid up the side of her throat and traced the curve of her cheek.

'You'd better be careful, doing things like that,' she said, and was fiercely proud of her level, amused tone. Inside, she was anything but level and amused. She felt as if she had suddenly awakened to find herself on a roller-coaster, just about to go over the first peak. 'I might take you seriously.'

Duncan's eyebrows raised. 'But my dear,' he pointed out, 'you told me yourself that I wasn't your type, so I was perfectly safe around you.'

She remembered. She also remembered how relieved he had been to get that news.

Now what, Mallory? she asked herself. You can't exactly tell him to quit——

'The shrimp Antoine,' Duncan told the waiter. Absentmindedly, he picked up Mallory's hand and toyed with her fingertips. 'The cucumber soup to start, and we'll have a look at the dessert trolley later.'

Mallory didn't hear a word of the discussion about the wine list, because by that time Duncan had raised her hand to his face and was gently rubbing the back of her fingers along his jaw.

As soon as the waiter had left, she said coolly. 'If you wouldn't mind giving my hand back, Duncan?'

He looked astounded to find her fingers clasped in his. 'Oh, I am sorry,' he said. 'I had no idea——'

'This is a public place. It's risky enough for a teacher in this town to be drinking wine with a man in public, but if I'm seen doing this sort of thing——'

He looked around. 'As dark as it is, how could anyone see?' he objected mildly, but he let go of her hand.

'After you've been sitting here for a while, your eyes adjust to the dark. And I really believe that a few people in this town make it a point to hang around at places like this, just to see who they can catch being indiscreet.'

'Rather unsporting of them. In a town this size, where else can lovers go?'

Her heart was thumping. Then she realised that, of course, he'd meant nothing personal. 'You have no idea how fortunate you are to be teaching at the college, where no one cares about your morals.'

The waiter returned with their wine, displayed the label, and pulled the cork, offering it to Duncan to sniff. The sample was poured into the glass; Duncan tasted it and nodded.

Then he said, 'I'll fill our glasses.'

The waiter blinked. 'As you wish, sir,' he said, making it plain that he wasn't responsible for patrons who wanted to look like fools.

'You've broken his heart,' Mallory said.

'Oh?' Duncan slid closer to her and tipped the bottle over her glass.

'Yes.' She was uncomfortably aware of the warmth of his body beside her, of the texture of his jacket against her arm, of the scent of his cologne. She forced herself to sound calm. 'The man was in heaven, with a customer who actually knew how the wine ceremony should be played. And then——'

'Then I had to go and spoil his fun,' Duncan said. 'Is it really that bad? Teaching at the high school, I mean?'

'Officially, what we do outside the classroom is our own business. But there are a lot of unmarried teachers here—I suppose it's because of the college—and every now and then someone kicks up a scandal. Usually, it's over nothing. Someone was seen leaving someone else's apartment at three in the morning after a date——'

'And chances are they were merely having breakfast together.'

'Or arguing politics.' She sipped her wine. 'And even if they were making love, for heaven's sake, what difference does it make? They're adults, and they were being reasonably discreet. It doesn't mean they'll advocate the same behaviour between the kids in their classes!'

Duncan smiled at her lazily over the rim of his glass. 'My point, precisely,' he said.

Mallory was lost. 'Which point?'

'That they're adults, and what difference does it make to anyone but the two of them?'

'Right. It's got nothing to do with anyone else.' As soon as she said it, she regretted it, because the devils were back in his eyes.

'Then it's all decided,' he said. 'We can't let our actions be dictated by the stuffy morality of the town.'

She swallowed hard. 'Duncan,' she said carefully, 'what exactly do you mean?'

'More wine, my dear?'

She shook her head. She was beginning to think that her first half-glass must have had something in it besides the wine. Her head was swimming.

'Of course,' he went on, 'we will have to be very discreet.'

'Discreet?' she croaked.

'Yes.' He added a little wine to her glass. 'In fact, I think we should get out of town altogether. How about it, Mallory? Will you come with me this summer?'

# CHAPTER EIGHT

MALLORY swallowed half a glass of wine without being aware of what she was doing. She wouldn't look at Duncan; she couldn't. The suddenness of the suggestion had caught her completely off guard, and she was unable to fight off the wave of sensations that flooded her.

No one who was watching them could have guessed at the confusion she was feeling, she thought. They must look like the typical couple, sitting a little closer together than most, perhaps, but with nothing about them to draw the attention of an onlooker. But Mallory was horribly aware of the warm pressure of Duncan's body against hers. They were sitting so close together that from hip to knee it seemed as if they were joined. Under the table, he had captured her hand again, and he was idly drawing circles with a fingernail on the delicate skin.

I never knew before that my fingertips were so sensitive, she thought. It's not fair, that he can do this to me in a public place. It isn't fair that he can do this to me at all—that he can hold my hand and make me imagine what it would be like if he made love to me——

She closed her eyes in an attempt to avoid the confusing reality, and knew instantly that it had been a mistake to think she could escape from her own imagination. The clarity of her mental picture stunned her. She could see quite vividly what making love with Duncan would be like. She could almost feel his hands caressing her body, his lips as they brushed fire on to her skin . . . A shivery feeling of danger tickled her veins. The egotism that so aggravated her would vanish, then, she thought, to be replaced by gentleness, by concern for her wishes and her comfort. For he was, essentially, a gentle man.

A whole summer with him... There would be no force, she thought, no coercion. He would use persuasion, and tenderness—and seduction, she reminded herself. And in the end he would get precisely what he wanted, and if that wasn't coercion, she'd never seen it!

This whole evening has been a seduction, and I almost fell into the trap, she thought. He made it all sound so plausible that I was nearly ready to toss my common sense out of the window to please him.

She was furious, as much at herself as at him. How could she have entertained the idea for an instant? Was she so dense that she didn't even recognise a con artist when she met one?

In any case, she thought, she couldn't go. Even if she wanted to—which she didn't, she told herself fiercely—there was Matt to be considered. The memory did not bring the relief that she expected.

'I don't know where you got the idea that I'd be flattered by this kind of proposition, Duncan Adams,' she said fiercely, 'but you're wrong!' She tried to tug her hand away.

He held on to it. 'It would let us finish the book,' he said. 'It seems to me that it's going to be impossible to complete it before the spring term is over.'

And it would be especially difficult to complete the work, she thought, if Duncan didn't want it to be finished ahead of his own self-serving schedule! 'I thought you said you made it a point never to get personally involved with anyone you're working with.'

'At the present rate of progress,' he disagreed, 'we can hardly call what we're doing *work*.'

That was certainly true, but it didn't make her feel better. 'Well, let me make this clear, Duncan. I have no interest in sleeping with you, now or ever——'

His forehead wrinkled with puzzlement. 'Did I say anything about us sleeping together?'

She was dazed, as if she'd just been hit in the solar plexus with an axe. 'You—didn't mean that?' she stammered.

He smiled at her. 'Oh, I'm more than willing. In fact, I'm quite delighted that you've changed your mind about me being your type. It will certainly make the summer a more interesting one.'

She was trying to breathe, but she couldn't pull air into her lungs. It felt something like the time she'd fallen from the top of the maple tree in the backyard on Armitage Road, and landed flat on her back on the ground. That's right, she told herself. Think of your childhood. Think of anything except the fact that you have just made a prize fool of yourself...

Duncan seemed to have thought the suggestion over. 'I think you're right,' he said. 'It might be very sensible for us to go to bed together. Once that mystery is removed, we could get back to some serious work on the book.'

Mallory sputtered, 'I'd sooner live with a gorilla than sleep with you!'

'Would you really?' He sounded mildly interested. 'It sounded to me as if you're looking forward to the idea just as much as I am.'

She stopped in mid-sentence and eyed him warily. The waiter brought their soup. Mallory said, tartly, 'Would you consider giving my hand back, Duncan?'

'Only if you promise not to slap me. Somehow I get the feeling that you'd like to, and so far I haven't done a thing to deserve it.' He released her fingers and picked up his spoon.

He was toying with her, she concluded. She had put her foot squarely in her mouth, and Duncan, with his devilish sense of humour, was enjoying it.

'I shouldn't have assumed that you were proposing an affair,' she said stiffly. 'I'm sorry. Can we talk about something else?'

'No, I rather like the subject you've chosen.'

It made her angry. Why should she be apologising to him, anyway? she asked herself. He was the one who hadn't made himself clear!

'Tell me, Mallory—was your outrage genuine?'

'What on earth do you mean? Of course I was outraged at the idea that you'd suggest I have an affair with you!'

'Why should you be offended?' he asked mildly.

She stared at him.

'I mean it. You're a very attractive young woman, you know. Why should you be upset at the idea that I'd like very much to make love with you?'

Mallory was speechless.

'Eat your soup,' Duncan suggested. 'It's really quite good.'

'You seem to think I should be pleased at the compliment you've paid me!' She picked up her spoon, half-consciously.

'I'd certainly like to know what you really think. I'm asking you to be specific, you see, because it's very difficult to tell whether you are genuinely insulted at the idea, or merely protesting loudly in an attempt to convince me—and perhaps even yourself—that you would never consider anything of the sort.'

She said, sulkily, 'I have no wish to discuss it further.'

'Very well,' he said equably. 'We won't.' He began to talk of music, and the professor of piano at Chandler, whose students would be giving a recital on Saturday night. 'We've got some very talented students over there,' he said. 'But the really exciting part of the evening will be the professor himself.'

Mallory had scarcely heard a word. If he didn't want to have an affair with her, she wondered, why had he suggested that she trail half-way across the country to be with him? They could finish the book in the autumn, or they could split up the work and rely on the mail. What need was there for them to be geographically close? 'Why?' Mallory asked suddenly.

Duncan's eyebrows elevated. 'Because he's such a tremendously good pianist himself,' he pointed out.

Mallory coloured. 'I wasn't talking about him,' she said finally. 'I was wondering—about this summer——'

'Why I want you to come with me?' The teasing note was gone from his voice.

She nodded, glad that at least he sounded as if he would be serious about it. If he had started to mock her again, she thought, she would have burst into tears and run from the room. She stared into the candle flame, afraid to look at him.

'You said that you wanted to get away from teaching home economics,' he reminded.

It surprised her. Of all things, that was the last one she would have expected him to remember and bring up. And what on earth did it have to do with whether she went with him? 'Not exactly,' she said. 'I'm not tired of home economics so much as I am of the high school. If I could finish my master's, and teach in a college programme——'

'Why limit yourself?'

She looked at him then, startled by the intensity in his voice.

He had put his spoon down, and he was tracing the delicate weave of the linen tablecloth with a fingernail. 'I thought, when you first handed me that manuscript, that you were like a fish trying to learn to fly,' he said. His voice was a little unsteady, as if he was finding words with difficulty. 'It seemed likely to me that you were attempting to do something that you had no talent or training for, just because you thought it looked easy.'

'It wasn't as easy as it looked, obviously,' Mallory murmured, remembering all the stacks of rewritten pages.

'Of course it isn't. But it soon became apparent that you have a gift, Mallory, and it doesn't involve trying to teach cooking and sewing to teenage kids who aren't interested. You're a born teacher, and you shouldn't be wasting your time with people who don't want to learn.'

She nodded, delighted that he finally understood. 'That's why I want to get to the college level.'

'But not home economics, Mallory!' He sounded frustrated. 'You have an intuitive grasp of morals and mores, of the dynamics of a group, of how the crazy pieces of society fit together... I'm afraid I'm not doing a very good job of making myself clear.'

'You can say that again. I haven't any idea what you're talking about, Duncan.'

He took a deep breath. 'Mallory, I think you're a natural sociologist. You need training, of course, but you have an instinct that we rarely see in beginning students.'

Mallory realised that she had eaten all of her soup without even tasting it. She stared at the empty dish and repeated the one word she had really heard, 'Sociologist?'

'That's right. Why did you end up teaching that class in independent-living, anyway? Was it assigned to you, or did you volunteer?'

'I asked for it,' she said absently.

'That's what I thought.' Duncan sounded very satisfied with himself.

She didn't say anything at all for a long time. The waiter took away her soup dish and replaced it with her entrée, steaming pink shrimp on a bed of rice. A small cup of clarified butter bubbled gently over the flame of a warming candle.

Mallory thought about what Duncan had said while she sampled her shrimp Antoine. He wasn't just making a pass at her, she was certain of that, now. He took his profession too seriously to joke about it. And she wanted to go. She wanted to toss aside all the practical concerns—Matt, her father, her responsibilities—and say yes, I'll go with you anywhere, Duncan. Anywhere at all.

But instead she shook her head. 'It's just not possible, Duncan. I simply can't leave here this summer.'

'I think you're missing the chance of a lifetime, Mallory. A chance to take a look at a new profession.'

'I'm awfully glad you brought it up,' she said. 'I hadn't thought of the possibility of changing fields at all, and you're right—sociology does rather intrigue me. It never did when I was in college, you know. I'll start looking into it——'

He interrupted. 'Your best opportunity for that is to come with me, you know. I won't be spending all summer in a dry, dusty library. There will be a lot of field research—some of which might be useful for your book, by the way. You could see what the job really involves— get a taste of the actual work and see if you'd like it, or if I'm out of line in suggesting it. You could pick up a class or two at the university, as well. There isn't a better department anywhere on the East Coast.'

His tone was cajoling, as if he was trying to persuade a baby that the contents of the spoon he was offering were really candy, and not medicine at all.

That wasn't quite a fair comparison, though, she told herself. She knew there would be plenty of work involved. He wasn't trying to disguise or sugar-coat that. And he was offering an unlimited opportunity to learn, to progress. It was flattering to find that he thought she had potential.

She sighed. It sounded so wonderful—spending a whole summer with Duncan, working with him, learning with him. She could probably learn more in a summer of practical experience than she could in a year of classroom study. And even if at the end of the summer she concluded that it wasn't the sort of career she wanted, she still would have lost nothing. It would be an experience that would strengthen her teaching next year.

It would be so easy to say yes, she thought, and to forget that she had responsibilities here, things that must be done and people who depended on her.

'I know all that,' she said, softly. 'But it doesn't change the fact that I simply can't go this year.'

'Why not?'

'I can't make any plans for the summer, Duncan. Dad's got a lecture tour set up; he'll be gone a great deal. And with Matt getting sick right now——'

'He's not dying, Mallory.'

'No, but mononucleosis can hang on for weeks or months. I can't just go off and desert him. I'm responsible for him.'

'And when are you going to start being responsible for yourself? Let Matt grow up, Mallory. He's not a baby any more.'

She was furious. 'But he's only sixteen! I am not going to turn my back on my brother, Duncan. As long as he needs me, I'll be here for him. And why you should think it's any of your business is beyond me!'

His eyes were unreadable. 'That seems to be the end of the discussion, then, doesn't it?' The words were pleasant, but his voice was edged with bitterness.

They fell into a silence that lasted through the rest of the evening, interrupted only by halting, laboured conversation. Mallory finished her shrimp Antoine, but it didn't taste very good. Funny, she thought. The first few bites had been wonderful.

Mallory slipped in the side door and went straight up to her room. The last thing she needed right now, she thought, was for Matt to start teasing her about Duncan. Or for her father to ask, in his absent way, how she had enjoyed the evening. The professor was quite capable of quizzing her for twenty minutes before it occurred to him that she might not have enjoyed herself at all!

I did, though, she reminded herself as she stood at the window, staring out through the leaded panes across the ravine behind the house. I enjoyed myself very much indeed until the question of how I would spend my summer came up. Then, everything had fallen apart.

Why? she asked herself. Why hadn't it been a simple matter of a question asked and answered, and that was the end of it? Duncan had made a very generous offer, and she had been forced by circumstances to refuse it. Why couldn't he have just accepted her answer, and gone on to enjoy the rest of the evening? Instead, he had acted as if she had rejected him personally, as well as the idea of working with him.

And why couldn't you have put it behind yourself as well? she asked herself suddenly. You could have changed the subject, brought up something else that might have eliminated the tension. Instead, you sat there like a fool, almost ready to cry, unable to agree to what he asked, and heartbroken because you had to tell him no...

I certainly didn't want to tell him no, she reminded herself. I wanted to go with him this summer, to work with him, to study with him——

To live with him?

The question echoed blankly in her mind. Was that why she had been so furious with herself for jumping to the conclusion that Duncan wanted to sleep with her—

because she'd been hurt when she realised that wasn't his primary purpose at all—only a pleasant afterthought?

Oh, come on, Mallory, she scolded herself. He couldn't have made it plainer that this wouldn't be a romantic holiday in the tropical islands. You'd be working your little head off to follow his programme—finish the book, take a few classes, hang around to observe his work, and get a little on-the-job training to see if you wanted to take it on as a career yourself...

Any one of those would be a full-time occupation, she thought. But with Duncan, they would all be not only possible, but fun. He had a way of challenging her to do more than her best, and the effort left her feeling an exhilaration that she hadn't experienced in years.

Besides, her traitorous mind reflected, not even Duncan could work all the time. And when the work was over—well, he *had* said that he would like very much to make love to her.

Her cheeks flamed at the thought. How could she even stand there and consider it? She must be crazy to think that she wanted to have an affair with Duncan Adams! She would be no more than one of the groupies who always collected around an attractive professor, lured by his personality instead of his subject. Was that what she wanted to be?

No, she told herself firmly. She *was* interested in the subject; she had proved that by her work on the book before Duncan had ever come along. But if she was to be totally honest with herself, was it only the intrigue of a new field to study that drew her?

Duncan was part of that attraction, there was no way to deny it. There was a magnetism about him that drew her as surely as if she was made of steel filings. All he had to do was to touch her, to hold her, to kiss her, and she was rocked by the delicious agony of wanting. Thinking about him made her feel that way even now, shuddering with the weight of her desire. Even though they had quarrelled at dinner, part of her had expected that he would kiss her goodnight—and all of her had been disappointed when he hadn't.

I don't want to let go of him, she thought. I don't want him to go away this summer. I'm going to miss him too much if he goes, she realised. He's crept into my life without me even noticing.

You really do want to have an affair with him, she told herself bluntly. And that, my dear, means that you positively should have your head examined!

Sociology. That was a safer topic for her thoughts. She had never considered the social sciences as a career field; she had never seriously thought about leaving home economics altogether. To make the switch now would require a great deal of time and effort. She had no idea how much, but she suspected that she had missed out on many classes, while she was in college, that would have helped her now. I'm crazy to even consider going back to being an undergraduate, she told herself, and Duncan is crazier to suggest it.

Well, she decided, in any case, there was no point in getting too concerned about it at the moment. She certainly couldn't do anything about it this summer; it would have been impossible even if Matt hadn't got sick. Someone had to be there to provide a watchful eye and a stable home for the kid.

For a moment, Mallory felt unreasonable resentment rise in her. It's not fair, she thought. Duncan's right— why should I have to give up what I want to take care of Matt?

Then she realised how selfish she sounded. It wasn't Matt's fault that he was sixteen years old. It hadn't been his idea to pick up this virus that might drag on for months. And, in any case, if she could just be patient, it would all be done eventually. Once Matt was through with school, Mallory would be free, and with her responsibilities honourably accomplished she could decide just what it was she wanted to do with the rest of her life.

'And in the next two years,' she told herself, 'I'll have ample opportunity to think about it!'

She had a sudden vision of herself in a cosy, book-lined room somewhere, looking up from a dusty reference volume to meet Duncan's eyes across a library table. Those coffee-brown eyes, which could sparkle with laughter or snap with anger or burn with passion——
He would get up from his chair and come around to her, and stoop to kiss the nape of her neck, and he would say, 'My darling, just looking at you drives me wild with desire to make love to you...'

Come on, Mallory, she warned herself uneasily. You're getting into fiction here, and pretty deeply at that!

A little more than two years, she thought drearily, and then I'll be free.

More than two years. Nearly a thousand days. it seemed to stretch out for ever, like an endless, deserted highway.

The scene in the big gymnasium was something close to panic. Melinda Anderson was standing in the middle of the floor, her hands on her hips. She was wearing bib overalls, and her hair was sliding out of the pigtails in which she had fruitlessly tried to confine it.

Above her, on tall ladders, two teenaged girls were hanging crêpe paper streamers. One would attach a loose end to a thin wire and then toss the roll of paper to the other, who would trim the length, twist the streamer, attach a new one, and toss the roll back.

Across the gym, two boys were rolling out flagstone-patterned paper over an arched bridge that formed a grand entrance to the ballroom, and a group of girls were blowing up blue and silver helium balloons to be attached to it.

'This is never going to be done,' Melinda muttered. 'And even if it is, it won't be worth looking at. Why we have to have the most formal dance of the year in the gymnasium is beyond me. We could rent the ballroom at the Country Club——'

'That costs money,' Mallory reminded.

'Allow me my dreams,' Melinda said with dignity. 'I have no desire to come into contact with reality this afternoon.'

'Besides, it will look wonderful in the dark. You've done a terrific job, and it's always a surprise to see how it turns out.'

'And look at the price I pay. Grey hairs and wrinkles. You're not the only one who's surprised when it comes off!'

'What's the theme?' Mallory looked around at the dark blue streamers concealing the steel rafters of the ceiling, the silvery stars hanging at random heights, the shimmery chandelier cover that looked just a bit like a moon, and the fake flagstone paths that wandered over the gymnasium floor between lattice-work gazebos.

'Can't you tell? That's the hardest part of all, you know—finding something that's recognisable, making sure that it's in good taste, and keeping a tight rein on the money so the whole junior class isn't bankrupt when the bills come in. The parents go through the roof at any idea that includes the word "night", because it might encourage their little darlings to come home with the morning newspaper——'

'I can't think why that should make a difference,' Mallory mused. 'They always do, anyway.'

'And Randy screams at anything that might contain a double meaning, and the kids hate everything that's left. I should have let them have their first choice this year.' She sounded horribly frustrated. 'They could have just borrowed potted plants from every florist in town, hung a few clouds, and that would have been it. We'd have been done in a couple of hours.'

'What was the theme?'

'"On Our Way to Paradise". The Garden of Eden didn't have crêpe paper streamers, you see. Or fancy light fixtures, either.'

'Randy hated it, I suppose?'

'He said this bunch of kids would probably put snakes in the potted palms. Or show up wearing nothing but fig leaves, which would be even worse.' Melinda put her head back and yelled, 'Let's move it up there if you want to have a dance tonight!'

'What are our other choices?' one of the girls hanging streamers said. 'I'm sick of this job.'

Melinda ignored her. 'Then their second choice was "Just Between You and I". I'm not even an English teacher, and I could see the fuss that would raise!'

Mallory made a gesture that took in the whole room. 'So what's this?'

'"One Enchanted Evening". Terribly unoriginal, don't you think?'

'The kids probably thought it was wonderfully new.'

'True. I forget that not everyone has attended fifteen proms, as I have. If you really want to help, Mallory, go corral the guys who were setting up the archway and have them start on the tables.'

'Aye, aye, sir.'

Two hours later, the seemingly impossible had been accomplished. The last streamer had been stretched neatly into place; huge murals replaced the scarred gymnasium walls with an atmosphere of mysterious night, and rows of potted plants lined the edges of the dancefloor.

Melinda stared at the soft drink can in her hand and said, 'I wish this was a vodka and tonic.'

Mallory laughed. 'No, you don't. You'd be flat on the floor asleep.'

'True. I haven't been to bed before two in the morning all week.' She yawned mightily.

'Shall I pick you up about eight o'clock?'

'I thought you and Randy——'

'He's bringing Caroline Adams.' Mallory kept her tone carefully neutral. 'He told me yesterday that she'd been able to swap shifts with another nurse, so she could take the time off.'

'Well, there's no accounting for taste. Thanks for the offer of a ride, but I'll have to be here early—I've scarcely got time to run home and change now before the parents start coming in to get the food ready to serve. Low-budget productions wear me out. Some day I'd like to sponsor a prom with a million-dollar budget.' She sounded dreamy.

'What would you do? Decorate the ceiling in diamonds?'

'Nope. I'd charter a plane and fly the whole bunch of kids to Paris. They could party at Maxim's, chaperoned by the flight attendants, and if they got out of line, there would be a security guard or two to take care of it. While I——' She yawned again. 'I would be at home in my own little bed——'

'Dreamer.'

'Exactly.' Melinda consulted her wristwatch and sighed. 'I've now talked away half of my make-up time. If I show up tonight with mascara on only one eye, it's your fault.'

Mallory drove home thoughtfully, glad that she wasn't the one who had the entire responsibility of the junior-senior prom. Melinda must enjoy it, though, she decided, or she wouldn't continue to take it on year after year.

Mallory arrived in the front hall on her way up the stairs at the precise instant that the doorbell rang. 'Damn,' she muttered. Melinda might have been exaggerating about cutting her schedule so fine that she had time to make up only half her face, but she hadn't been joking entirely. If anything happened to slow her down——

'Matt!' she called hopefully. 'Are you expecting a friend?'

He wandered out from the living-room. He had got dressed today, in worn jeans and a battered T-shirt, but he still looked drawn and tired. 'Nope,' he said. 'But I'll get the door.'

'Thanks! If it's someone for me, just say I'm running away from home and I'll send a forwarding address.' She started up the stairs. 'Are you supposed to be dressed?'

'Caroline said she thought I'd feel better if I wasn't lying around in pyjamas all the time.'

'Oh. Well, I suppose Caroline knows best. When did she tell you that?'

'She stopped by this afternoon.' The front door opened, and Mallory, at the top of the stairs, heard him say, 'Wow! What made you get into that kind of rig?'

'I understand it's the expected uniform for the occasion.'

Mallory groaned. Duncan! The last thing she needed right now was Duncan. She supposed he wanted to work on the book tonight. Damn Duncan anyway; there was no predicting him. She would just go up to her room and get dressed, and she would deal with Duncan later, she decided. Surely he'd be reasonable, when he saw that she had every intention of going to the dance.

'Well, no girl will ever get me into one of those,' Matt announced. 'You look sort of like a penguin.'

A penguin? Despite her resolution, Mallory found herself leaning over the banister so she could peek down into the hallway.

He didn't look like a penguin. He looked like a very tall, very handsome, very self-assured man in a well cut black tuxedo, and for an instant Mallory couldn't get her breath.

Duncan laughed. 'Wait and see,' he advised. 'By next year, you'll not only be wearing one, you'll be matching it to your date's dress.'

Matt didn't sound convinced. 'You didn't. Mallory never wears black.'

You idiot, Matt, she thought. Jumping to the conclusion that he's come here to take me to the dance, when obviously he just stopped by on his way—to what? What other formal event would be going on in this city tonight? The piano recital at the college, she remembered. She bit her lip against the twinge of disappointment that swept through her.

'I know,' Duncan said kindly. 'We older folks get by with breaking the rules now and then. What colour is she wearing, by the way? Not that it really matters. I brought white orchids for her, just to be on the safe side.'

Mallory gulped. The nerve of the guy, she thought. I didn't invite him. I never said a word to him about this dance. And I don't want him!

The heck you don't, she thought, with colour burning to her hairline. You want him so badly that you'd do nearly anything to have him. You don't care a bit how he got here, or why. None of that matters any more. Not the book, not the quarrel you had, not the fact that he's going away and you're staying. The only thing that counts is that he's here, and that you can share tonight with him. One enchanted evening, alone with the man you love.

Slowly, things began to make sense. She hadn't been jealous of Caroline that night at the theatre because Randy had noticed and admired her. She had been jealous of her because she was with Duncan. Even then, Mallory told herself, deep down inside, you knew that you wanted him. Even then, it was more than just attraction.

You idiot, she thought. How could you have fallen in love with Duncan Adams?

# CHAPTER NINE

MALLORY tried to talk herself out of it the whole time she was dressing. It was impossible, she lectured herself, to fall in love with a man she had only known for a matter of weeks. It was not only impossible, it was insane to let herself believe that such a thing could happen. And it was idiotic to think she could actually love a man like Duncan Adams, anyway.

She catalogued his faults while she took her shower. He was arrogant. He seemed to think that he knew everything. He found nothing odd about taking over her schedule, making plans without bothering to consult her. He expected her to devote all her time to this deadly book.

'That's not quite fair,' she told herself. 'After all, it's your book, Mallory. You started it. But, as long as you're being honest, you may as well admit that without him it would never be done.'

That was one point in his favour, she was forced to acknowledge. She hardened her heart, however, and continued to list his flaws, and by the time she got out of the shower she had herself well in hand. No woman could love a man whom she could dissect so dispassionately, she congratulated herself.

That attitude lasted till she was standing at her wardrobe door in her lacy underclothes, staring at the dress she had planned to wear tonight. It was the perfect garment for the chaperon at a teenage dance; it was demurely cut, with a long, full skirt, puffy sleeves and a simple neckline that cried out for a single strand of pearls. It was pale blue, sprinkled with tiny pink and yellow flowers. It was a pretty dress, simple and ordinary.

And Mallory didn't want to be ordinary tonight.

That was why she found herself plunging into the back of her wardrobe, in search of the garment bag which held the flotsam of her wardrobe. Here were the clothes she had bought but could never bring herself either to wear or to dispose of. The problem with most of them was that there was no place in this city to wear them. That was especially true of the dress she was thinking of now...

The dress was fuchsia, the deep pinkish-purple that so few women could wear without looking as sallow as a lemon. That, she thought, was why it had been marked down so far on the sale rack. On Mallory, the colour was dynamic, bringing blue-black highlights to her hair and mysterious shadows to her eyes. It was not the colour which had put this dress into the bag at the back of the wardrobe, but the style. It had looked quite appropriate in the little dress shop but, once home in her bedroom, Mallory had written it off as far too daring.

At first glance it looked quite ordinary. It was made of a soft, sheer fabric that draped gently about her; the bodice front was gathered to a neck band which rested snugly at the base of Mallory's throat. On the band she pinned her grandmother's cameo brooch, and the diamond setting twinkled against the shimmery cloth. The dress looked almost prim, until an observer realised that it had no sleeves, no shoulders and no back—just the long, full skirt and the bodice front demurely gathered to the throat.

When she came downstairs a little later, even Matt's eyes were ready to pop. 'You're going to freeze in that gym,' he announced with all the scorn a sixteen-year-old could muster. 'Silly things, girls.'

And Duncan? she wondered. Did Duncan think it was a silly dress? She didn't want to look at him. Why was he here, anyway? What had made him come? Had Caroline felt sorry for her? Or Randy? She stared at his mirror-polished shoes, watching miserably as he crossed the room to her.

A warm hand cupped her chin and gently raised her face to his. There was a glow in his eyes as he looked down at her that sent the hot blood rushing through her veins, and prickles of delirious anticipation flashed through every cell.

'Why are you here?' she asked, so softly that she could scarcely hear. Instantly, she regretted the question. I don't want to know she told herself. I just want to enjoy tonight.

'When Randy invited Caroline, he told her you'd invited me. I thought you'd just overlooked telling me about it.' Then the bantering note died out of his voice, and he added, unsteadily, 'I'm here because I couldn't stay away.'

She looked up at him, and slowly held out her hands. He clasped her fingers in his. It was a sort of vow exchanged between them.

'It won't be very exciting for you,' she murmured.

'I think I can find all the excitement I need.'

For a long moment they stood and looked at each other, and Mallory forgot how to breathe, for the caress of Duncan's eyes was more intimate than any touch could have been.

'Gee,' Matt complained. 'If all you do at a prom is to stand around and stare at each other like this, I'm not going next year.'

Mallory smiled tremulously.

'He'll change his mind when he grows up,' Duncan said huskily. 'I brought you flowers, but I'm not quite sure what to do with them.' His fingertips brushed her bare shoulders. 'I can't pin them here.'

She fastened the orchids carefully at her waist. But she wasn't thinking about the flowers. She was remembering the look in his eyes, and the fiery touch of his hands...

It was a warm, soft April night, unseasonably mild. As they crossed the pavement, dim figures in pastel gowns and tuxedos filed into the school. There was no horseplay now, no loud voices. For many of these kids, Mallory thought, it was the first time they had ever been so formally dressed, and their proper manners sat as uncomfortably as the bow-ties did.

The football player greeted them at the door. 'Good evening, Miss Mitchell,' he said, 'Hello, Dr Adams. Welcome to "One Enchanted Evening".' Then he grinned, and his formal manners slipped. 'Where did you leave the baby?'

'Her grandfather is babysitting,' Duncan said. 'He spoils her rotten, of course. She's very difficult to handle after she's spent any time with him, but of course grandparents do have certain rights.' He urged Mallory into the gymnasium, now a softly lit ballroom.

'He's not, you know,' she murmured.

'I suspected that.'

'I forgot all about her in the hurry of getting ready, and her basket is still on my dressing-table. I meant to take it down to Dad's study——'

'I'm sure if he hears her crying, he'll pick her up. In the meantime, you owe me one for pulling you out of trouble.'

'One what?' she whispered.

Duncan smiled. 'I'll think of something—later.'

They danced, and ate, and chatted with Randy and Caroline for a moment; then drank punch, and took their turn at patrolling the school grounds and car park to nip any trouble in the bud.

'It seems a waste of time,' Duncan mused as they strolled through the grounds. 'There's hardly a bush out here to hide behind.'

'There usually isn't much of a problem at the prom, because everyone is on his or her best behaviour. But at one of the other dances a couple of years ago we had to break up a gang fight.'

'Kids are charming, aren't they? I'm sure Alexandra will never give us any trouble of that sort.'

'I shouldn't think so,' she said drily.

'Though I am a bit concerned that she doesn't seem to gain any weight,' Duncan went on.

There was no point in letting that line of conversation continue, Mallory thought, and changed the subject. 'Of course, it usually isn't fighting that we're looking for out here.' Her light shawl slipped a little, and she stopped in the shadow of the building to straighten it.

'No?' Duncan pretended shock. 'Do you mean, kids might actually slip out here for a—a hug?' He sounded horrified, 'Or maybe even a—I can't bring myself to say it.'

Mallory giggled.

'Obviously,' he said, 'a lady like you doesn't understand the seriousness of what I'm talking about. I'll have to demonstrate what I mean, because I can't possibly explain it.'

'You don't have to demonstrate anything to me,' Mallory said hurriedly. 'I know what a kiss is, that's certain——'

He shook a finger at her. 'I'm shocked at you, Miss Mitchell. To let such a word cross your lips! It calls for appropriate disciplinary action——'

His hand closed on her arm and drew her further into the shadow of the building, where a big tree overstretched the path. He leaned against the tree, and pulled her against him.

She was off balance, tingling, sharply aware of the hard length of him through the sheer dress. Her shawl slipped off her shoulders and trailed to the grass. The texture of his sleeve was rough against her bare back as he held her firmly close.

The first touch of his mouth against hers was tentative, almost questioning—as though he was making an experiment. Mallory sighed and let her hand slip up over the slick satin lapel to rest against his neck. Her fingers lay lightly over the pulse point. Was his heart pounding a little unsteadily, she wondered muzzily, or was it her own that was fluttering so, sounding like a tom-tom in her ears?

Then he kissed her again. This time he was neither tentative nor questioning; there was a gentle command in the way he held her, a self-assurance that would not be denied.

He raised his head, finally, and looked at her. 'God, I want to make love to you,' he said. His voice was hoarse. Her heart skipped a beat, and then resumed its fierce pounding. He kissed her again, more gently this time. In the dimness of the shadows, she couldn't see the expression in his eyes, but she couldn't miss the ragged humour in his voice when he said, 'Maybe the kids aren't such fools, after all, Mallory.'

'Do you mean—kissing in the shadows?'

'Careful,' he warned. 'I'll have to take steps again to keep you from saying that word.' A lazy finger traced the edge of her bodice; Mallory tried to still her shiver. She had never known before that her shoulders were an erogenous zone!

The April breeze was cool against her flushed face. 'Which word?' she asked innocently.

'You're a tease, Mallory Mitchell. How long does this affair continue?'

'Dawn. They dance till two in the morning, then they go play miniature golf, then they have breakfast at one of the restaurants——'

'And you're on duty all night?' His arms tightened a little, as if he was reluctant to let her go.

'Till the bitter end.' I wish I wasn't, she thought. I'd go with you tonight without another thought, because I love you so.

Just as well, she thought, that it was impossible. By morning, reason would surely have reasserted itself. Love wasn't enough, by itself—especially when it meant turning her back on responsibility.

He sighed. 'That's what I was afraid of.'

'You don't have to stay for it all,' she whispered.

For a moment, she was afraid that he'd agree. Then he seemed to shake off the sober concerns. 'And miss the miniature golf? I'll have you know I'm a mean miniature golfer.'

It warmed her heart that he was such a good sport about it. Not many men would have found an event like this entertaining, even considering the stolen moments in the shadows. But Duncan seemed to be having a good time, despite the juvenile company, the unspiked punch, and the fact that his companion had to spend a great deal of her time watching the kids instead of staring soulfully at him.

And that was probably just as well, too, Mallory told herself. All the wise words that she had recited to herself all evening had made no difference. She had fallen in love with him, and at the moment she was foolish enough not to care if the whole world knew it.

She told herself firmly to stop thinking about it. One enchanted evening—tomorrow she would worry about where to go from here.

Duncan was right; he was deadly on the miniature golf range. Mallory was grateful for the excuse that her long skirt kept getting in her way, but she knew that even in jeans she wouldn't have stood a chance.

They put away a farm-style breakfast at the restaurant, and said goodbye to the kids. Then Duncan drove her home, slowly, through the last of the darkness.

They sat in the car for a little while, neither of them wanting the night to end. Finally, Duncan ran a hand over the back of his neck and said, 'Mallory, about this summer——'

'Not now,' she pleaded. 'We'll talk about it later. Not tonight . . .'

'It isn't night any more,' he said. 'Look.'

To the east, a fiery glow lit the sky. As they watched, the golden sun seemed to lift away from the horizon with an effort, and the hazy dimness of early morning seemed to burn away before their eyes.

'Mallory——'

She was panicky, suddenly terrified of what he was going to say. Not now, she thought. We'll fight again, and all the enchantment will be gone. I can't let that happen—I won't let that happen.

'Come to tea this afternoon,' she said, quickly.

'You don't want to talk about it, do you? But we will have to, Mallory, sooner or later.'

'We'll talk about it at tea,' she said. It was a pleading promise.

Duncan sighed. After a long moment, he said, 'I'll see you later, then.' He kissed her lightly, as if he was preoccupied.

By tea time, she told herself, I have to decide what I'm going to tell him. Stay? Go?

But she knew better than to think she had any choice at all. There was only one thing she could do.

'And Duncan isn't going to like it,' she muttered under her breath as she climbed the stairs to her room. 'He isn't going to like it one bit.'

That's fair enough, she added to herself. I don't like it much, either. But it's the only thing I can do. He'll go away this summer, and I'll stay here. In the fall, when he comes home . . .

Then we'll know, she thought. I'll know if I'm really in love with him, or if I've only let my imagination run away with me. A summer isn't so long, after all. Three short months, and he'll be back . . .

It felt like for ever.

He didn't wait for tea time. He showed up on the back doorstep a little before noon, wearing jeans and an open-necked shirt. He didn't bother with greetings. 'Let's go on a picnic,' he said.

Mallory shook her head. She was spooning ingredients into a casserole dish, and she'd lost her place in her recipe. She found it again, added a sprinkle of garlic salt and covered the casserole with a sigh of relief. 'Can't,' she said. 'I simply haven't time to put together a picnic lunch today.'

Duncan frowned. 'The lunch is in the car,' he said. 'I invited you; therefore I provide the food.'

She looked up, surprised. 'Well, you don't need to sound furious about it,' she said. 'I'm sorry, Duncan, but I have my whole afternoon planned.'

'And you've very conveniently planned it so there isn't time to talk to me,' he said, evenly.

'Of course I haven't. I'm getting meals ready to put in the freezer for Dad and Matt this week, and then after that it will be time to start the scones for tea, and then——'

'Don't you realise that's part of the problem?'

'What do you mean?'

'You learned to cook,' he pointed out. 'Why can't Matt? Some day he'll be on his own, and he will have to eat. Why must you take care of every single meal in this house, whether you'll be here to help eat it or not?'

She looked up at him, stunned into silence by the depth of anger in his voice. 'All right,' she said finally. 'If your picnic is so important to you, hang on to your hat for a couple of minutes while I clean this up, and then I'll come. Will that satisfy you?'

'I've run into your definition of a couple of minutes before.' He went to the doorway. 'Matt!'

'Yeah?' Matt put his head out of the living-room.

'Be a good guy and clean up this mess in the kitchen as a favour to me, will you? I'm going to take your sister out and talk some sense into her.'

'Oops,' Matt muttered. 'I don't think I like the sound of that.' But he came into the kitchen.

'That dish goes in the freezer, Matt. The hamburger gets browned and put in——'

Duncan handed her a jacket and took her arm. 'He'll figure it out, Mallory,' he said. 'It will either be right or wrong, but it will get done. Come on.'

'You're a bully,' Mallory muttered.

'That's right. I don't want my fried chicken to get cold.' He started the car and pulled out of the driveway fast, as if he half expected she would try to jump out and return to her work.

'You made fried chicken?'

'No. The take-out place down the street did.'

'That doesn't count.'

He sent a searching look at her, and turned his attention back to the street. 'That's a great deal of the problem, Mallory. You seem to have the idea that no one else can do anything as well as you can, and so therefore you try to do everything.'

'Did something specific bring on this attack, or are you just down on me in general?' Mallory asked. She was trembling inside. How could the gentle man of last night have become this angry, driven person?

'I thought perhaps it was just the book that was causing all the trouble,' he said. 'I hoped that once it was done, you'd relax a little. But I've come to the conclusion that it won't make any difference. You never rest, do you?'

'Of course I do! And as for the book being finished, you're the one who insisted that the whole thing be done over. It would be completed if you'd let me do it myself!'

He was grimly silent, his jaw set. Mallory thought about it, and decided that what she had said was a dirty blow.

'Sorry,' she muttered. 'I'm not dumb enough to believe I could have done it on my own. I shouldn't have said that.'

He didn't answer. Gravel spun from under the car's wheels as he stopped at the edge of the park. He got a blanket and a wicker basket from the back, and said, 'Come on.'

'Look, Duncan, isn't a picnic going to be a farce when we're fighting like this?'

'We're not fighting,' he said. 'We're discussing our future.' He started off down the path.

She almost had to run to keep up with his long stride. 'Do we have one?' she asked, soberly.

'That's what I want to find out.'

He spread the blanket in a patch of sunlight on a sloping hillside. Above them, a maple tree was beginning to show the pale green of new leaves, and in the hollow below a few brave jonquils flaunted their yellow crowns. On the far slope, a couple of kids were playing tennis.

It was so peaceful, Mallory thought. A lovers' picnic in the park—and she was going to have to destroy it, sooner or later.

'I can't go with you this summer,' she said.

He didn't seem to hear. He was spooning baked beans on to a paper plate. He added a crunchy chicken leg and a mound of potato salad, and handed it to her. 'Can't?' he asked calmly. 'Or won't?'

She was furious; it seemed to her that he didn't want to understand. 'Can't,' she said crisply. 'I have a responsibility to Matt——'

'Matt is a big boy. He's capable of doing far more than you think he can.'

'Matt is sixteen years old! That is far too young to be left on his own for summer unsupervised. If you had seen some of the things I have, things that go on when parents let their teenagers have too much freedom——'

'He has a father, Mallory.'

'Yes, he does. And you know my father——'

'Yes, I do. But do you, Mallory? Do you really know him?'

'What does that mean?' Absently, she picked up the chicken leg and began to nibble at it. 'Dad's an absent-minded scholar. He'd never notice what Matt was up to, as long as it didn't interfere with his book.'

'Do you think he'd really allow Matt to run wild? He's a scholar, certainly, and he's quite capable of forgetting what time it is when he's chasing a new idea. But be truthful, Mallory. Haven't you spent the last few years encouraging him to do that?'

'I did what had to be done. When Mother died, Dad was lost! He didn't know what to do—he was in shock——'

'But what about now? Did it ever occur to you that the professor may be burying himself in the books because you've taken over the responsibility for Matt, and left him with nothing to do? Did you ever think that he might *like* having his son depend on him?'

It hadn't. She stared at him, the chicken leg suspended in mid-air, her mouth open.

'They need me,' she whispered.

'Do they? Or is it you who needs to be needed? You like being Saint Mallory, don't you? You enjoy it when everyone feels sorry for you and talks about what a wonderful job you've done and how generous you are to give up so much to take care of your brother.'

'Stop it!' she cried.

'Why? Does the truth hurt? Well, Matt's growing up. When are you going to start taking care of Mallory?'

'I can't be so selfish,' she said. 'I can't walk out on my promise, and if you really cared about me, Duncan, you wouldn't ask me to turn my back on my brother!'

'I'm not,' he said. 'If Matt didn't have a father, or if he was handicapped, or if he was eight years old, I wouldn't be saying these things. But he's a young man, Mallory. It's time you let him start to learn how to act like one.'

'By leaving him on his own all summer, while I go off to have an affair, and Dad travels from college to college giving his lecture series? What kind of loving care is that, Duncan?'

'It might be better than the smothering kind he's getting now.'

'And what are you going to say if it turns out that he can't handle that responsibility? Are you going to shrug your shoulders and say, "Gee, I guess I was wrong," when he starts taking drugs or wrecks a car while he's drunk or gets a girl pregnant?'

'Do you really think you could prevent those things, if he was determined to do them?'

She stared at him, and said finally, levelly, 'I know that I would blame myself if I wasn't here.'

He shrugged. 'Then I guess that's the end of it. I won't bother you with it again.'

The emotionless tone of his voice frightened her more than any degree of anger could have. I need him, she thought. I want to spend my life with him. 'You don't understand, Duncan! I want to go with you.' Suddenly she was desperate to make him understand. 'I'd go in a minute——'

He was reaching for her, with a light in his eyes that was not so much triumph, she thought, as it was fierce gladness.

'If it wasn't for Matt,' she whispered, and hated herself for wiping that joy from his eyes.

'You're using Matt as a shield,' he said. 'An excuse.'

He turned away, and packed up the remains of the food with a taut economy of motion. Mallory sat silent on the corner of the blanket and watched.

'It would be no wonder if I did,' she said, finally. 'What are you asking me for, anyway, Duncan? I'm confused. Why should it surprise you that I haven't jumped at your offer when I don't even know what it is? Do you want a co-worker? A student? A lover?'

'All of those things,' he said, low-voiced. 'Every one of them, Mallory. And more. I want a chance for the two of us to find out what we really mean to each other— if we want to spend our lives together.'

It took her a long moment to comprehend what he had said, and then joy burst inside her like the sparkle of fireworks. It was more than she had even hoped for...

'It's only for the summer,' she whispered. 'I can't leave Matt this summer. But when you come back in the fall——'

'Next fall, Matt will still be sixteen,' he said. 'And he will still—according to your rules—need you.'

'Not all the time,' she said. 'He'll be in school. You mustn't think that I watch him every minute, Duncan. I've got more sense than that! But in the summer there is so much time to get into trouble, and with Dad gone for weeks on end... Next fall,' she said, and her voice was a pleading whisper, 'when you come back—we'll have all the time in the world, then.'

Duncan stretched out on the blanket on his back, and put his forearm over his eyes. 'That's just it,' he said, heavily. 'I've been offered another job. I won't be coming back at all.'

For a moment, she thought she hadn't heard him. 'But you're the head of the department!'

'Also almost a one-man department. It's not my style, Mallory. I had to try it to know for sure, but I don't like it.'

'So what will you do instead?' She felt as if the world was rocking under her.

'I've been offered a teaching position at the university I attended. I'm going to take it.'

'But to go back to that, after heading the department——'

He sighed. 'Administration is not what I want to do with my life, Mallory. I'm a teacher and a writer, not an organiser or a politician.'

'It's a step backwards, Duncan.'

'Not as far as I'm concerned. Chandler is fine for your father. He's a pure scholar, and he could do his work anywhere, as long as there was a place to prop up a book. But I can't. I need the atmosphere of a busy campus, and the freedom to specialise instead of trying to do everything. I've spent too much of my time this year on paperwork. It's smothering me.'

She pleated the edge of the blanket between nervous fingers. Her head was spinning. She had been so sure that in the fall, free of the heaviest of their obligations, they would have time to explore each other and their desires for the future. There was no need to hurry into a decision, she had thought. Instead, suddenly, there was no time at all.

He had fallen silent, his arm still across his eyes. She couldn't see much of his face, but she could see the tension lines around his mouth.

'I understand how you feel about Matt,' he said. 'But—dammit, Mallory, surely there's a way...' He didn't sound angry any more, just sad, and very tired.

Suddenly, she needed to be close to him, to be held and consoled. She crept up beside him, and his free arm pulled her down to him, snuggling her close until her head rested on his shoulder. There was nothing passionate about this embrace; it was simply the expression of two human beings caught in a situation they could not escape.

They didn't speak. Slowly, the peace of the park crept over them. The gentle breeze toyed with Mallory's dark hair, the birds sang in the maple tree above them, the scent of the flowers draped them like a blanket. And, finally, they slept, nestled close, as if they were trying to shut out the world.

When she woke, she was stiff from the hard ground, but her head was much clearer. 'There has to be a way,' Duncan had said, and perhaps he was right. They would find it, together, if they looked hard enough.

She shifted and stretched, and Duncan said, 'Did you have a nice nap?'

'Very good. It's gotten a little chilly, hasn't it? Have you been awake long?'

'A while. But I didn't want to disturb you. You were so tired.'

Mallory yawned. 'I'm not used to being up all night, that's sure. What time is it?'

Duncan twisted and looked at his wristwatch. 'A little after five.'

'Five o'clock?' She was horrified. 'I've missed tea!' She struggled out of his arms and jumped to her feet, brushing her fingers through her hair. 'Take me home, Duncan. I didn't have any scones made, but perhaps I could still——'

'What's the hurry?' He sat up, slowly. 'They'll manage.'

Something snapped, deep inside Mallory. She turned accusingly on him, and said, 'You planned this, didn't you, to try to prove something to me? You knew perfectly well that I wanted to be home in time to make the preparations for tea, and when I fell asleep you deliberately let me sleep through——'

'I thought you needed your sleep a great deal more than the hangers-on at your house needed scones, yes. If that's what you're accusing me of, I plead guilty.'

'Well, thank you very much, Dr Adams! Next time I want your interference, I'll ask for it. Now if you would take me home——'

'Gladly.' He didn't speak until they were back at the house on Armitage Road. When Mallory reached for the door-handle, he leaned across her and caught hold of it. 'Just a minute,' he said. 'I've got one more thing to ask you.'

'Make it fast.'

'Why didn't you marry the jerk who thought you should make a home for some deserving man?' he asked. 'You might as well have, Mallory. What you're doing now is every bit as crazy. You have no more personal life than you would have if you'd married him. Less, actually, because this way you have a full-time job, too. You're just as much confined by your own inflexibility as you would be by his version of the marriage vows. You cook and clean and sort socks and have dinner on the table every night at seven. Only this way, you don't have the fun of making love once in a while, or the satisfaction of holding your own child in your arms.'

'That's enough, Duncan!'

'When are you going to wake up, Mallory Mitchell? Are you going to wait till——'

She put her hands over her ears. 'Stop messing up my life!' she cried. 'Just stop it!'

There was a long, harsh silence. 'Very well,' Duncan said. He released his hold on the door-handle and leaned back in his seat. 'Enjoy your tea, Mallory.'

She thought, as she slid out of the car, her ears still ringing with the words she had screamed at him, that she heard him say, 'Enjoy your life...'

## CHAPTER TEN

THE living-room was quiet and neat, but the murmur of voices drew Mallory to the kitchen. She walked in just in time to see her father snap a dish-towel at Matt, who chuckled and moved out of range.

'Hi, Mallory,' the boy said. 'You missed a great new kind of cookie. Caroline showed me how to make them, and they really tasted good. But we ate the whole batch.'

Caroline rinsed the suds from a baking sheet and set it off to the side to drain. She smiled at Mallory. It was a little hesitant, Mallory thought, as if she was apologising for being caught in another woman's kitchen. She shouldn't be afraid I'll be offended, Mallory decided, when actually the shoe was on the other foot entirely. Caroline had done her a favour.

'Sorry I didn't make it back in time,' she said.

'No problem.' The professor picked up the baking sheet and started to dry it. 'None of us felt up to your standards at tea, so we made a pot of coffee instead. With Caroline's cookies and half a cake that Matt found in the freezer, nobody went hungry.' He turned to Caroline. 'Don't you think everyone had a good time?'

She nodded. 'People don't come here just because of the food, anyway.' Her voice was soft. 'It's such a friendly house, Mallory. They come because you've made it a pleasant place to meet new friends.'

It should have been reassuring, Mallory told herself, but somehow it wasn't. 'Did you have a crowd?'

'Not a lot. Melinda was here,' the professor said. 'Randy Craig dropped in, but he had to leave. A couple of people wanted to talk to you about your dinner party on Saturday.'

'Your fund-raising dinner?' Caroline asked.

'Yes. I'm rather glad I wasn't here. It's supposed to be a surprise.'

'If you need any help in getting ready——' Caroline offered.

'I'd love some.' Mallory poured herself a cup of coffee. 'Can I help?'

'It's mostly cleaned up,' Caroline said. 'Besides, we made the mess—we can clean it.'

'That's a healthy attitude,' the professor agreed. 'Listen to the woman, Matt.'

Matt groaned theatrically and winked at Caroline.

Not Matt too, Mallory thought. Apparently men of all ages toppled like tenpins for Caroline Adams! She'd better warn Matt that Caroline wouldn't be around much longer, she decided. It was obvious already that he would miss her when she left.

Caroline wiped the stainless steel sink carefully. 'Hal,' she said, casually, 'I'd like to talk to Mallory a minute.'

'Hmmm? Oh, of course.' He looked like an abashed schoolboy. Even his ears were red. Perhaps, Mallory thought, I shouldn't worry so much about Matt— perhaps Dad is the one I should watch out for!

'Matt, a little homework would be a good idea,' the professor told him.

'Can I go back to school tomorrow?' Matt bargained. 'I feel great.'

She wanted to tell him that they'd call the doctor tomorrow, and see what he said. But before she had a chance to speak, the professor had put his arm around Matt's shoulders. 'Oh, I think you can try it for half a day,' he said as they went off down the hall.

'Thanks for stepping in for me,' Mallory said. 'I'm sorry to impose on you like that, when you've already been such a great help with Matt.'

'I enjoy Matt. He's a remarkable young man. He's getting much better, too. I think in a month or so he'll be good as new.'

A month, Mallory thought. Not as bad as she had thought it might be, but nevertheless——Oh, Matt, she thought, why did you have to get sick right now?

Caroline put a small box on the table. 'I found the lovebirds I was telling you about—you know, the blown glass ones that Duncan brought me from Venice years ago. I'd like you to have them.'

Mallory shook her head instinctively, and then thought, I certainly can't explain to Caroline why I don't want those damned lovebirds! I can't tell her that I won't be able to look at them, because every sight will remind me of the man who brought them home. And it would hurt her terribly if I rejected them without an explanation. So I'll have to accept them graciously, and make myself think of Caroline instead of Duncan when I look at them. I'll think of how generous Caroline is...

She unwrapped the tissue paper that cushioned the delicate ornaments and set them on the table. The fragile glass was paper-thin, and the hand of an artist was apparent. It looked to Mallory as if the birds had been captured and frozen in motion.

One of them was nestled, wings folded, feet tucked, ready to settle in for the winter. The other had extended his wings, ready to fly. His neck was arched and he was looking down at his mate, as if to see whether she would follow.

That's Duncan, she thought, ready to go, and yet waiting for a sign. But, unlike the lovebird, he would not wait for ever.

And as for the other bird—someone has to stay home and take care of the nest, she thought.

She looked up at Caroline with a smile that was only slightly forced. 'Thank you,' she said. 'I'll treasure these always.'

'I thought you might enjoy them.' Caroline refilled her cup. 'I always liked looking at them. See how happy she looks, now that her mate has come back to her?' She pointed at the bird with the folded wings.

Funny, Mallory thought, that the two of us can look at the same thing and interpret it so differently.

'You don't look tired from last night,' she said. Randy and Caroline had still been at the restaurant when she and Duncan had left, waiting for the last teenager to give up and go home.

Caroline laughed. 'I slept all morning. I'm used to working odd hours, so it was nothing unusual for me to be up all night. Did you have a good time?'

It was a tentative question, Mallory thought, as if Caroline was afraid of hearing the answer. Then she realised why the question had been asked. Caroline wasn't dumb. She must have suspected, when she saw Mallory with Duncan, that the original plans had gone awry. This was a sort of apology for walking off with Mallory's date.

'As much fun as one can have, under the circumstances,' she said. A little shiver ran through her at the memory of those all-too-brief moments under the shadow of the huge tree, when Duncan had been kissing her. 'Randy's a nice guy, isn't he?' She tried to make it a friendly question, hoping to persuade Caroline that she was not in the least bit jealous.

It worked; at least, Caroline seemed to relax. 'Very nice,' she agreed. 'It was quite an interesting evening.'

What did that mean? Mallory wondered. But Caroline didn't seem inclined to continue. 'Are you going to miss your job at the hospital?' Mallory asked. It was aimless conversation, meant to bridge an awkward pause.

Caroline's eyebrows raised. 'I hadn't planned to give it up. Why?'

'But I thought—surely you'll be going with Duncan?'

'He's told you he's going back East, then?'

'Yes.' Mallory knew she sounded a little defensive. But why should she? Surely there was an obvious reason for him to have told her that! 'We'll have to finish the book by mail, I suppose.'

'I see. I'm sorry to hear that.' Caroline sipped her coffee.

Why had she said that? Mallory wondered uneasily.

'It will make it difficult to finish the work, I'm sure,' Caroline went on, and Mallory relaxed. 'No, I'm not going with him. It will sound silly, I suppose, because I lived here for so many months and didn't become involved in community activities at all. But now that I've started meeting people and doing things, I feel more at home here than I've ever felt in any city. Duncan understands that. He's been very generous, but for a man of Duncan's age to be living with his sister—well it has certainly put a cramp in his life-style!'

I know, Mallory thought. If he hadn't had a roommate, that afternoon in his apartment would have ended up quite differently. She found herself wishing that he had taken her to bed that afternoon. Now, she might never share that with him. He might never make love to her—never again tease her about Alexandra—never share, as he had in those rare moments, his love of his work and his dreams for the future. For he would be gone.

It's only temporary, she told herself. But two years, she had to admit, didn't sound temporary. It sounded like for ever.

'There has to be a way,' Duncan had said that afternoon.

Well, there isn't, Mallory told herself. You've got to stop banging your head against the wall searching for something that isn't there. You will just have to be patient.

'I think a year of Duncan's life devoted to me is enough, anyway,' Caroline was saying. 'It's time for me to stand up for myself.'

'I'm afraid I don't understand.'

Caroline looked down into her coffee-cup and sighed. 'I did some very foolish things,' she said. 'The crowning touch was thinking I was in love with a doctor at the last hospital I worked in.'

'Oh,' Mallory said softly.

'He didn't love me, of course. Duncan took the job at Chandler mostly to get me away from there. Now that I've been here a while, I've grown to love it. There are some very special people in this town.' She looked just a little flushed, and determined, and a little embarrassed.

And suddenly Mallory understood why Caroline didn't want to leave. No wonder neither Randy nor Caroline had seemed in a hurry to get out of that restaurant this morning; they, like the kids, had not wanted the night to end.

Mallory said, with a sudden flash of humour, 'And one particularly special person, I think you mean?'

Now the flush was definite. 'Well, yes, now that you mention it. He understands what it feels like to have been hurt, and he's helped me.'

'It's none of my business, of course, but—do I hear wedding bells in the distance?' Mallory teased gently.

Caroline bit her lip. 'Not immediately, but we've talked about it. Would it bother you, Mallory?'

Mallory was honestly shocked. It wasn't as if she and Randy had ever had an agreement, after all! 'Of course not. He's not my property, you know.'

Caroline's face lit suddenly, as if a candle had been set afire behind her eyes. She jumped up and bent over Mallory's chair to give her an impulsive hug. 'Oh, my dear,' she said. 'I'm glad that you don't mind—I've worried so about it!'

That sounded like Caroline, Mallory thought—always concerned about the feelings of others. She asked, curiously, 'Doesn't it bother you a little—that he was married before?'

Caroline shook her head. 'No.' she said, solemnly. 'That's history, you see. And it's part of what made him the man I care so much about. I wouldn't want to take that experience away from him.'

Yes, Mallory thought, Randy was a lucky man. Caroline was not only a beautiful woman, but she had the rare quality of really caring about others, of wanting to make them happy. Randy would be pampered and loved, and in return, he would adore this rare jewel of his...

She ran a gentle finger over the smooth glass ornaments. 'Perhaps you should have the lovebirds back.'

Caroline smiled. 'I don't think I need them any more. And they'll fit so beautifully into your collection. I must be going home, because I have to go to work at eleven tonight. It was the only way I could get last night off.'

They will be happy, Mallory thought. She picked up the fragile lovebirds and carried them upstairs to arrange them on her dressing-table. Pairs, she thought, bleakly. I collect them, but it begins to look as if I'll never be part of one. Everywhere there are couples, and I'm alone...

Stop feeling so darned sorry for yourself, she accused. It was your choice—a choice you had to make.

She thought about the summer, and how very much she wanted to be with Duncan. She wanted to share everything with him—his life, his work, his love. She turned the lovebirds to look more directly at each other, and then picked up the fragile eggshell that lay in the wicker basket at her elbow, her painted-on eyes closed and the single dark curl lying heavily on her forehead.

Was it still possible, she wondered, that she and Duncan might some day make a life together? That some day they might even have a real Alexandra?

I want to give him everything, she thought. Why couldn't he understand? He had turned away from a life he wanted, for Caroline.

Yes, she reminded herself, but he didn't exactly wrap her in tissue paper. He didn't try to heal her, he just brought her to a place where she could heal herself. It's different, Mallory.

'There has to be a way,' Duncan had said.

'There is,' she murmured, trying to convince herself. 'When Matt is gone from home——'

Two years. And what would happen in those two years? she wondered. Time wouldn't stop for Duncan; he would be teaching, learning, growing.

And what about me? she thought. In two years, I'll still just be Mallory Mitchell, home economics teacher. I'll be older, and more tired of my job. But I won't be any closer to learning what I really want to do with my life. I won't have changed or grown.

Will Duncan even want me, then? We'll be two different people in two years, she thought, with terror striking deep into her heart. We have a chance now to grow together. But if we let this chance go by, will we ever be able to get it back?

She thought it over for two solid days. The weight of the eggshell in the basket grew heavier and heavier, she thought, as she carried it back and forth to school. Alexandra seemed to have become the symbol of the weighty decision she must make. But it didn't seem that there was any other choice. She couldn't just turn her back on Matt.

And yet, could she bear to turn away from Duncan, either, knowing that she might never see him again?

Finally, she went to her father. The professor was in his study, as he usually was in the late afternoon, with the desk-lamp casting a pool of light over the blotter and striking silver sparks off his hair. A book lay open before him, and when he looked up there was the barest trace of impatience in his eyes.

But it died away as he saw her standing there, nervous fingers pleating the edge of her sweater. He pushed the book aside.

'Daddy, can I talk to you?'

He raised an eyebrow. She hadn't called him that in years, she realised. Funny that the childish name had slipped so naturally to her tongue now.

He pushed his chair back from the desk, and Mallory slipped to the floor beside him and laid her cheek against his knee. It was easier to confess something, she had learned long ago, if she didn't have to look him in the eye while she did it.

'I'm feeling very selfish right now,' she whispered.

His hand rested on her head and stroked the length of her hair.

'I feel awful about asking this,' she said, 'but I want so badly to go with—to go away this summer. And yet, there's Matt to be considered. I know he's not grown up yet, by a long way. And I promised Mom that I'd watch out for him. But——'

'But what you want now won't allow you to keep your eye on Matt.' His tone was gentle.

She nodded, miserably, and wiped a stray tear from her eyes. 'I wondered if—if it can't be worked out, Dad, I'll understand. I know you've got this lecture tour all summer. But I thought that maybe sometimes Matt could go with you. Or perhaps Melinda would come and stay while you're gone. Or—or even Caroline. He likes her a lot. I know it would be tough this summer, but in the fall he'll be in school——'

'What you're really trying to convince yourself of,' the professor murmured, 'is that Matt will be all right without you.'

'He's feeling better. He really is. But it would be a lot more work for you.' Her voice was hesitant. 'And I did promise Mom that I'd look out for him——'

'I think you've forgotten something, Mallory.' His voice was stern, and Mallory shivered. She hated it when her father spoke to her in that tone of voice. 'You've forgotten that your mother was very ill when she extracted that promise from you.'

'I'm not trying to back out of my promise,' Mallory whispered.

'Yes, you are. And you should. Mallory, your mother's judgement wasn't the best towards the end, when she asked you for that promise. And mine hasn't been very good since, when I've allowed you to carry that load. It's been very convenient for me to have you here, and I've told myself that it didn't really matter anyway, because you were happy here. But you're obviously not contented any more.'

'I feel so guilty for wanting to go away,' she murmured.

'Mallory, you've done a wonderful job for the last few years, and your mother certainly wouldn't want you to sacrifice your own happiness for Matt's sake. Or for my convenience, either.' He stroked her hair. 'You want to go with Duncan?'

She nodded meekly. 'How did you know?'

'It's been no secret at the college that he hasn't been happy here. The two of you are very much alike, you know. There will always be one more goal to be reached, one more challenge to be met, one more thing to be learned——'

She laughed, shakily. 'Perhaps you're right.'

'I know I'm right. You care very much for him, don't you, my dear?'

She swallowed hard and looked up at him. 'I love him, Dad. More than I ever thought was possible.'

He was smiling. 'Then go with him, my dear.'

'You really don't mind?'

'We will miss you, of course. You've spoiled us, Mallory. But life is a one-way street. Once you've passed an intersection, you can't turn back and take it later— even if it turns out that it was the only right way for you to go.' He patted her head and added firmly, 'But don't sit here crying on my knee. Go and find your young man and tell him you're ready to start packing.'

It wasn't as easy as the professor seemed to think it would be. Duncan seemed to have vanished off the face of the earth. He wasn't in his office; he wasn't at home; he didn't—as she had half hoped he might—show up for independent-living class. The week dragged on, and by Saturday Mallory was reduced to begging information from Caroline.

They were sitting at the kitchen table chopping vegetables for the dinner party when Mallory said, trying to sound casual, 'What's Duncan been up to these days? I haven't seen him around lately.'

'Oh, nobody's seen much of him. He's been up at the university for a couple of days, because they had some resources in the library that he couldn't get here.'

'Oh.' Mallory didn't know whether to be relieved or disappointed; at least she knew now that he wasn't trying to avoid her—or was he? He could have called me, she thought. He could have told me he was going. But why should he? She had told him to stay out of her life. What if he had made up his mind to do just that?

She got up to stir the soup, which was simmering gently on the back burner. What if he no longer wanted to see her, or have anything to do with her? If so, she thought, it really shouldn't surprise her. They hadn't parted on pleasant terms. And, after all, Duncan had never said anything about loving her. Perhaps, after the demonstration of her shrewish temper on that Sunday afternoon, he had decided he was better off without her.

For the first time, she began to feel afraid. 'Life is a one-way street,' her father had said. Had she unknowingly passed by the crossroads that she was so certain now was the right one for her?

'Would you like me to give him a message?' Caroline asked.

'Oh, no,' she said. 'It wasn't important.' She had her back to Caroline. For a moment, she held her breath, wondering if the woman would pursue the subject.

Caroline didn't. 'How do you keep everything straight?' she asked. 'Twenty-four for dinner, and you don't even look flustered.'

'Wait till you see me at eight o'clock, when we start serving. That's when it gets to be a juggling act.'

Matt came in. 'Here's the extra copies of the menu, Mallory. I put one at each place. The tables are all set up.'

'You look tired, Matt,' Caroline observed.

Mallory looked over her shoulder. Under Matt's cheeky grin, his face was pale, she noticed.

'Yeah, a little,' he admitted. 'We had to haul all the furniture around to make room. Dad went to pick up the extra chairs. Did you want me to fold the napkins special?'

'Have you considered working on a nap instead?' Caroline asked pointedly.

'Caro, I'm too old to take afternoon naps.'

'Then don't. But it looks to me as if you'll collapse just in time for the party, if you don't rest a while now.' She turned back to the vegetables as if she didn't care what he did.

Matt groaned and turned on his heel. One minute later Mallory heard the stairs creak as he climbed them. She could hardly believe her ears.

Caroline picked up a copy of the menu. 'I would never have enough nerve to try something like this,' she said. 'Seven courses would be about six too many for me.'

Mallory shrugged. 'In the old days, they served fourteen. Of course, those were the days of venison pies, and whole partridges, and——'

'Servants,' Caroline finished. 'Butlers and foot-men——'

'I have servants,' Mallory said with a smile. 'You and Matt and Melinda to serve, me in the kitchen, and Dad to take care of the wine. What more could a modern woman ask?' She was up to her elbows in veal, spreading the cutlets with savoury filling and rolling them tightly.

'How long have you been working at this?'

'A week. Actually, the menu is easy—most of the work can be done ahead of time.'

'And you don't even get to have fun at your own party.'

'Not the fund-raisers. Somebody has to stay behind the scenes and do the work.'

The telephone rang. 'I'll get it,' Caroline offered, and went out to the hall without waiting for an answer.

Mallory was almost glad of the reprieve. Caroline was wonderful help, but it was peaceful to be alone in the kitchen, with no observant eyes to see if her mask dropped for a moment. She would have to see Duncan when he came back, she knew. For her own peace of mind, she had to tell him she was sorry. And then, if he rejected her apology—what then?

Caroline came back in with an air of determination, dusting her hands. 'That,' she said, 'was Melinda. She's picked up a beastly head cold, and she doesn't think your guests would appreciate having her sneeze on them tonight.'

Mallory's head suddenly started to pound. 'She can't do this to me!' she wailed. 'They'll be arriving in two hours——'

'Well, she did it. Never fear, I've——'

'We'll have to find someone else. No one can handle serving more than one table; I've cut it fine as it is. Who——'

'Mallory, I'm trying to tell you that I've already taken care of it.'

Sudden suspicion surged over Mallory. No, she thought, you've just got Duncan on the brain. Caroline must have called Randy. He'll do; at least he can put the food on the table.

'I called Duncan,' Caroline added. 'He's on his way over.'

Mallory said, faintly, 'I thought you said he was gone.'

'He came back today. Perfect timing, don't you think?' Caroline was so proud of herself for having solved the problem that Mallory didn't have the heart to hurt her feelings. But all she wanted to do was put her head down on the counter and cry. I can't face him tonight, she thought. Not here, not now! In less than two hours her house would be filled with twenty-four hungry guests. There would be no time to talk, no chance of so much as a private word.

And that may be why he agreed to come, she told herself bleakly. After all, the last thing she had told him was to stay out of her life. Duncan was coming to help wait tables because his sister had asked a favour, not because he had any desire to talk to Mallory. If she, rather than Caroline, had called him, she thought dismally, he'd probably have told her that if she wanted to have parties of this sort, she should expect to do the work herself...

Don't be silly, she told herself. Surely he wouldn't set foot in this house if he was still angry with me. He couldn't have changed his mind so quickly, anyway. Just last weekend he wanted me to go away with him. And when I tell him that I've talked to Dad, and I can go—when he finds out that I want to go—then everything will be all right.

The veal was finished, ready for cooking, by the time Duncan came. Caroline had gone upstairs to change into her plain black dress; Mallory was wiping the kitchen counter and trying to make a list in her head of the order in which things must be done. But the only thing she could think of was Duncan. How would he look, what would he say?

He was in the kitchen before she heard anything at all. She turned to find him watching her. Try as she might, she could see no expression in his coffee-coloured eyes. His voice held only calm friendliness. 'Caroline says you need a hand,' he said, coolly.

Mallory was confused. If he had been angry, it would not have surprised her. But this unruffled composure was beyond her understanding. Surely he could not be calm about this! Unless——

Unless it just didn't matter to him any more, no matter what she did.

Mallory had the sudden sensation that the room had become a carousel that had gone crazily out of control, revolving faster and faster, spinning dementedly until she wanted to scream.

She did not. She turned away instead, and rinsed her dishcloth in hot water, and said, her voice perfectly steady, 'Thanks for helping out.'

'You didn't know that she called me.' It was not a question. 'Do you want me to leave?'

Yes, she thought, I want you to go. Getting through the evening will be strain enough, without having to see you, and know that it was all a mistake. I need time to pull myself together. And yet... 'No,' she whispered. 'Don't go, Duncan.'

Painful as it would be, she knew, she would have to face up to it some time. In his few days away from her, he must have discovered that he didn't care for her. That was the only answer, she thought. If he had loved her at all, he could not have looked at her with that detached calm, like a mere acquaintance.

'Dad's in the dining-room,' she said. 'He'll tell you what he needs help with.'

He accepted his dismissal calmly, with only the twitch of a muscle in his jaw showing that he even realised he had been dismissed. He turned on his heel and left the kitchen, and Mallory sagged against the sink, too hurt even to cry.

I should be glad, she thought fiercely. I should be glad to know that I meant no more to him than that. If he can take it so calmly, then I know it wasn't really me that he wanted—only someone to have an affair with. All those lovely things he said about my talents and my potential—he's probably said them to a hundred women. I should be glad that I didn't get caught in that trap!

But she wasn't glad. She wasn't glad at all.

The guests trickled in. The professor passed the tray of wine-glasses, and reported to Mallory that it was a good crowd. 'There's a lot of giggling going on already,' he said. 'They're curious about what you've come up with this year.'

'You do this regularly?' Caroline asked in horror. She was sitting on the corner of the kitchen table, sipping a glass of wine—to calm her nerves, she had said.

'Mallory does everything,' Duncan said.

Was there a bitter twist to the words? Mallory wondered. Or had it been just her imagination, that under the smooth voice lay pain? Don't let yourself hope, she thought. 'I'm getting a little tired of it,' she admitted. She stirred the sauce that would be poured over the veal, and said, 'The appetisers are ready.'

'Is that a hint?' Caroline asked. She drained the wineglass.

'I'll move them into the dining-room,' the professor said. 'Matt, if you want to start hauling trays out——'

'Lay on, Macduff,' Matt said. He looked more cheerful, Mallory thought, after his nap. They'd been right—all the people who kept telling her that Matt was growing up. She hadn't wanted to see. Now that she had begun to look, however, she was growing to like the outlines of the young man she could see emerging.

'Very good, Matt. There may be hope for modern education yet,' the professor murmured, and vanished to round up the guests.

For the moment, Duncan and Mallory were alone. She wouldn't look at him. Instead, she turned to stir the soup, and in her awkwardness splashed the scalding broth over the back of her hand. She tried to swallow her cry of pain, but in an instant Duncan was beside her, pushing her over to the sink and holding the injured hand under cold water to soothe the burn.

The pain in her heart was far worse than that in her hand, she thought miserably. And being so close to him, with his arm around her and her head almost resting on his shoulder, did nothing to ease the ache. She looked up at him. He was inspecting the damage to her skin, but as if he felt the weight of her gaze he turned his head and stared down into her eyes.

'Why did you have to come back?' she whispered, and when she saw the pain that flamed in his eyes, she took a tiny, scared breath, afraid of what she had released. Then there was no time to think because his mouth came down on hers, fiercely, with a driven, desperate demand. The burn on her hand was forgotten; the only thing that existed was their two bodies, and the urgency of their need for each other.

'I hate to interrupt, Clyde,' said a polite voice from the doorway, 'but I've served the appetisers to your table. Mallory, Dad says he'll need the first tureen of soup in five minutes.'

She tried to pull away. Duncan's arms tightened like a steel cable around her. 'Thank you, Matt,' he said. Then he looked down at Mallory, and said, low-voiced, 'I came back because, God help me, I couldn't stay away.' He let her go then, and followed Matt back to the dining-room.

Suddenly her heart was screaming with happiness. He does still want me, she thought. He does!

'We have to talk,' he said when he came back with the empty soup dishes. 'I have to explain——'

Caroline came in, laughing. 'This is great fun,' she said. 'I begin to see why you think it's worth all the work.'

Duncan scowled at her and picked up a plate of salmon mousse.

'What's the matter with him?' Caroline asked as the door closed behind him.

I wish I knew, Mallory thought. She felt as though she'd been clubbed. What was there for Duncan to explain, after all? Surely if there were explanations, it was she who should be making them——

The veal was served and removed, and the salad. Mallory's brain was spinning, still desperately trying to figure out what Duncan had meant. There was no chance to ask him; whenever he came to the kitchen, Matt or Caroline or the professor were already there. When it came to the time for the strawberry Bavarian cream, though, a miracle occurred. Mallory looked up and realised that they were alone.

'I was wrong,' Duncan said, rapidly. 'I was selfish, and obstinate, and mean, and——'

'No,' she said. 'Obstinate and selfish, yes, but never *mean*——'

'Yes, mean. You have a right to your feelings, and I forgot that your overactive sense of responsibility is one of the things that makes you special. I still don't think Matt needs you as much as you think, but if that's what you have to do to be satisfied, then I'll wait——'

'I don't.'

'You what?'

'Dad and I have worked it out. You were right; they can get along without me. If you still want me, I'll come with you.'

'If I still want you?' His tone was incredulous. He reached for her.

It was all the answer Mallory needed, and she had enough presence of mind left to know that if he kissed her she would forget everything else. 'Duncan,' she said, softly. 'Shut up and take the Bavarian cream to the dining-room before the guests come looking for it, all right? We'll talk about it later.'

'You can bet we'll talk about it some time,' he promised, sounding frustrated. 'If this evening is ever over. Damn dinner parties, anyway.'

'No more,' she said. 'Not like this one, anyway.'

She stood quietly in the centre of the kitchen for a long moment, after he was gone, waiting for regret to strike her. Surely she should feel fear, or second thoughts about committing herself to him. But all she felt was trust, and a deep sense of the rightness of what she was doing. She loved him, and in some way or other, she was sure, he loved her too. That was all that mattered now.

Duncan was back in record time. And when the professor came in a few minutes later to get the fruit and cheese tray, he said, mildly, 'Don't let me interrupt you,' and went out again without having been noticed at all.

Matt, a few minutes after that, was less discreet. 'I hate to break this up when you're obviously having such a good time,' he announced, 'but the guests would like to applaud the cook, and Dad says you have to come out and say goodnight. Do you suppose they'll leave tips?' he added hopefully.

Mallory laughed, a little shakily.

'Make a note to yourself,' Duncan said, looking down at her. 'We want an apartment with no neighbours. And this kid is not to have the address or the phone number.'

'Gosh,' Matt said, sounding a little hurt. 'You'd think I'm too young to understand what's going on.'

The formality of the party had collapsed after dinner, with the waiters joining the guests. Caroline was stretched out in a chair with the professor sitting on the arm; one of the guests was toying with scales at the piano, the others were absorbed in conversation. When Mallory came in, a ripple of applause swept the room.

She bowed theatrically. 'I'm glad you enjoyed it,' she said. 'It's the last time, you see.' For an instant, regret gripped her.

Duncan seemed to feel it. His hand closed gently on hers, and he said, softly, 'For now. You'll do this again, somewhere, if you want. You're just not going to keep on doing everything for everybody else—right?'

She smiled up at him. 'Right.'

The professor gestured for quiet. 'I think, since we have all of our dearest friends assembled here, that perhaps it would be a good time for an announcement,' he said.

Mallory froze. Daddy, she thought, you can't do this to me! You can't make an announcement of something, when Duncan and I aren't even sure what we're going to do!

The professor looked down at Caroline, who nodded.

'I'd like to introduce you to the newest member of the Mitchell family,' he said. 'Caroline, bless her warm heart, has decided that she will only be happy as the wife of a Shakespearean scholar. And, as you know, I'm not dumb enough to argue with a beautiful woman when it is definitely to my advantage to agree with her. So——'

The buzz of congratulations drowned out even the drumming of blood in Mallory's ears. Her father—and Caroline? But——

She and Caroline were side by side on the doorstep as the last guests walked away. 'I thought you were talking about Randy,' Mallory said, finally.

Caroline looked stunned. 'Are you upset, Mallory?'

'Upset? No. But—the prom——'

'I only went because Hal was being stubborn. He said no woman my age should tie myself down to a man like him, and that I didn't know what I was missing by refusing to date other men. So I went to the prom with Randy, and then I told Hal that if that's what I was missing, I'd just as soon be dead, and if he didn't marry me I'd picket the administration building at Chandler and tell the world that he had toyed with my affections and then thrown me over.'

'She made her point,' the professor conceded. He put his arm around Caroline.

Mallory thought that she had never seen her father look quite so happy. Perhaps this wasn't such a mad idea, after all, she decided. 'When's the wedding?'

'Soon,' Caroline said. 'We're certain, so what's the point in waiting? Mallory—you don't mind, do you?'

'Not if you don't expect me to call you Mom.'

Caroline laughed. 'I'd much rather call you sister,' she said, with a knowing look up at Duncan.

Mallory gave her an impulsive hug. 'I owe you so much,' she whispered. 'Bringing him here—and now, taking on Matt——'

Caroline laughed. 'Just in case you start to wonder some day whether I sacrificed myself for you and my brother, I had decided I wanted Hal long before I ever met Matt.'

'I'm glad. Very, very glad.'

Duncan took her arm, possessively. 'Mallory and I are going for a walk. All that heat in the kitchen, you know——'

'Yeah,' Matt said. 'I saw some of it, and it was pretty hot.'

'Go to bed, Matt,' his father told him.

Matt seemed to be taking the new order of life calmly, Mallory thought. The last doubt about whether she was doing the right thing had vanished. 'I left a mess in the kitchen——' she said.

The professor shook his head. 'Never mind. Caroline and I will clean it up. It'll get us into practice at being old married folks.'

Duncan took her hand. Suddenly shy, she walked along the driveway with him, down to the deserted street. Moonlight washed across the lawns of the sleeping neighbourhood. Only the Mitchell house was lighted still. The breeze was cool against her flushed cheeks, and suddenly she shivered.

'Cold?' Duncan asked softly. 'Would you like my jacket?'

'No.' She forced herself to laugh. 'They're both very conservative, aren't they? I mean, Dad didn't even ask about our intentions, and Caroline just assumed that we'll be getting—married—too.' Her voice broke, just a little.

'That's conservative, all right.' He sounded a little uncomfortable.

'Did it surprise you?'

'Not exactly. Caroline didn't confide in me, but I had my suspicions.'

They walked along in silence. He had slowed his pace to fit hers, and her hand nestled comfortably in his. But the rest of her wasn't comfortable. Why are we doing this? she asked herself. We came out here to talk, didn't we? So why don't we talk, dammit? Even if it's only little stuff——

'You would have enjoyed independent-living class yesterday,' she said. 'The kids were talking about what they've learned from living with the eggs so far. It's been interesting, I must admit. I didn't think I'd get much out of it——' Her voice trailed off. Dumb, Mallory, she told herself. Very, very dumb. Can't you think of anything better to talk about?

'What have you learned, Mallory?' He sounded as if he really wanted to know.

'That I'm not ready to have a baby yet,' she said, thoughtfully. 'That I need to learn to balance my own needs with those of others before I take on a job like raising a child.'

'Do you want to know what I learned?'

'You've hardly had Alexandra at all,' Mallory said.

'That's exactly the point. I learned that I don't like the idea of being an absent father. I want to be married to the mother of my children. You see, Mallory, I'm pretty conservative, too. I'm sorry if that sounds un-necessary to you, but it's very important to me.' He stopped and swung her around to face him. 'We've had such a very little time,' he said. 'But it only took a couple of days without you, and I knew that this summer won't be enough. Can you trust me enough to take a chance and marry me?'

She couldn't answer.

'I wash my own socks, you know. I'm not a terrific cook, but I'm willing to learn. And while I would like to have an Alexandra call me Daddy some day, I'm quite willing to wait till you're ready——'

His words seemed to be an echo of something she had heard before, and then she remembered telling him about the man who thought she should devote her life to making a home for some deserving male. He had re-membered very well indeed what she had said she didn't want in a marriage!

'I'm sure, you see,' he said. 'Very, very certain. But if you aren't——Well, I love you too much to give you up, no matter what.'

'I'm sure, too,' she whispered. 'I couldn't ask for any-thing more from life than you, Duncan.'

Their kiss was a vow in itself, a pledge made.

But she was uneasy still. 'I can't make guarantees,' she said. 'I know you think that I'm meant to be a so-ciologist, but what if I don't like it, Duncan?'

'Then you'll do something else,' he said easily. 'You don't think I'm doing this to gain a co-author, do you? I can get into that kind of trouble without adding mar-riage to it.' Then he sobered. 'I want to marry you be-cause you're the woman I love,' he said. 'If we're partners in other things as well, that would be a bonus.'

'How can I turn down that kind of deal?' she teased. 'Why did you agree to help me write the book, anyway?

Obviously it wasn't because you didn't have anything better to do.'

'Because it was a good book.'

She looked doubtfully up at him.

'And because I wanted to see you again,' he admitted. 'I thought the book would be safer than asking you out to dinner—you couldn't spill the manuscript all over me.'

'Why, you——'

'I didn't know I was going to fall in love, Mallory Adams.'

'Mallory Adams,' she said thoughtfully. Mrs C. Duncan Adams. What *does* that "C" stand for, anyway?'

'Crazy-about-you,' he murmured, and kissed her again.

'If it turns out to be Clyde...' she began, and then there was a long pause.

'If it's Clyde, what?'

She giggled and threw her arms around him. 'Then I'll marry you anyway,' she said. 'And count myself lucky.'

The moonlight seemed to shine on them in blessing as they walked hand in hand down Armitage Road.

# Harlequin Presents

## Coming Next Month

**1111   AN AWAKENING DESIRE  Helen Bianchin**
Emma, recently widowed, isn't looking for romance. But a visit to her late
husband Marc's grandparents in Italy seems like a good first step in picking up
the pieces of her life. She certainly isn't ready to deal with a man like Nick
Castelli!

**1112   STRAY LADY  Vanessa Grant**
Since her husband's death, George has felt that she doesn't belong anywhere
anymore. Then Lyle rescues her from her smashed sailboat and makes her feel
at home in the lighthouse. But to kindhearted Lyle is she just another stray?

**1113   LEVELLING THE SCORE  Penny Jordan**
Jenna had once loved Simon Townsend—a mere teenage crush, but he has
never let her forget it. So when she has a chance for revenge, she takes it.
Simon, however, has his own methods of retaliation....

**1114   THE WILDER SHORES OF LOVE  Madeleine Ker**
She'd never thought it would happen to her—but almost without knowing it
Margot Prescott turns from a detached reporter of the drug scene to an
addict. Adam Korda saves her. But the freer she becomes of the drug, the
more attached she becomes to Adam.

**1115   STORM CLOUD MARRIAGE  Roberta Leigh**
Sandra has always known Randall Pearson. He was her father's faceless deputy,
and has only once surprised her. One night he asked her to marry him. She'd
refused then, of course, but now four years later Sandra is doing the
proposing!

**1116   MIRACLE MAN  Joanna Mansell**
Lacey is happy with her safe, sexless relationship with her boss—Marcus
Caradin of Caradin Tours. Then he asks her to go on a business trip with him.
Suddenly, in the exotic surroundings of India and Nepal, it isn't safe
anymore....

**1117   ONE CHANCE AT LOVE  Carole Mortimer**
Dizzy's family background made her wary of commitment. Zach Bennett is the
first man to make her want to throw caution to the winds. But her position is
awkward. Because of a promise, she has to conceal her real nature from Zach.

**1118   THERE IS NO TOMORROW  Yvonne Whittal**
Despite her plea of innocence, Revil Bradstone despises Alexa because he'd
once caught her in a compromising situation. Now he threatens vengeance
through her employer. Desperate, Alexa is ready to promise him anything!

Available in October wherever paperback books are sold, or through
Harlequin Reader Service:

In the U.S.
901 Fuhrmann Blvd.
P.O. Box 1397
Buffalo, N.Y.  14240-1397

In Canada
P.O. Box 603
Fort Erie, Ontario
L2A 5X3

# Temptation™

## TEMPTATION WILL BE
## EVEN HARDER TO RESIST...

In September, Temptation is presenting a sophisticated new face to the world. A fresh look that truly brings Harlequin's most intimate romances into focus.

What's more, all-time favorite authors Barbara Delinsky, Rita Clay Estrada, Jayne Ann Krentz and Vicki Lewis Thompson will join forces to help us celebrate. The result? A very special quartet of Temptations...

- **Four striking covers**
- **Four stellar authors**
- **Four sensual love stories**
- **Four variations on one spellbinding theme**

All in one great month! Give in to Temptation in September.

TDESIGN-1

# Harlequin Superromance

---

**Here are the longer, more involving stories you
have been waiting for... Superromance.**

Modern, believable novels of love, full of the complex
joys and heartaches of real people.

Intriguing conflicts based on today's constantly
changing life-styles.

Four new titles every month.
Available wherever paperbacks are sold.

---

# ATTRACTIVE, SPACE SAVING BOOK RACK

Display your most prized novels on this handsome and sturdy book rack. The hand-rubbed walnut finish will blend into your library decor with quiet elegance, providing a practical organizer for your favorite hard-or soft-covered books.

*Only $9.95*

***Approximately 16" x 8" when assembled***

***Assembles in seconds!***

------------------------------------------------

To order, rush your name, address and zip code, along with a check or money order for $10.70* ($9.95 plus 75¢ postage and handling) payable to *Harlequin Reader Service*:

Harlequin Reader Service
Book Rack Offer
901 Fuhrmann Blvd.
P.O. Box 1396
Buffalo, NY 14269-1396

*Offer not available in Canada.*

BKR-1A

*New York and Iowa residents add appropriate sales tax.

## HARLEQUIN SIGNATURE EDITION

### VIOLET WINSPEAR
### HOUSE OF STORMS

Editorial secretary Debra Hartway travels to the Salvador family's rugged Cornish island home to work on Jack Salvador's latest book. Disturbing questions hang in the troubled air over Lovelis Island. What or who had caused the tragic death of Jack's young wife? Why did Jack stay away from the home and, more especially, the baby son he loved so well? And—why should Rodare, Jack's brother, who had proved himself a man of the highest integrity, constantly invade Debra's thoughts with such passionate, dark desires...?

Violet Winspear, who has written more than 65 romance novels translated worldwide into 18 languages, is one of Harlequin's best-loved and bestselling authors. HOUSE OF STORMS, her second title in the Harlequin Signature Edition program, is a full-length novel rich in romantic tradition and intriguingly spiced with an atmosphere of danger and mystery.

**Watch for HOUSE OF STORMS—coming in October!**

HOFS-1